A Different Mary

Anne Rayment

Christian Focus Publications Ltd.

Published by
Christian Focus Publications Ltd.
Tain   Houston
Ross-shire   Texas

© 1989 Christian Focus Publications Ltd.
ISBN 0906 731 95 X

Printed and bound in Great Britain

Contents

Contents continued

Dedicated to:

Chas, Anna and Rebecca

Chapter 1

Dread-full-ness

Mary, who was thirteen years old when this story begins, was walking home from Mass on a grey, sunless Sunday morning in February. With her were her two younger sisters, Meggie and Joanne, and a French au pair, in her twenties, who was called Danielle.

They were smartly turned out, as befitted a Sunday morning. Meggie, blonde, plump and looking younger than her ten years, clasped the hand of the four year old Joanne, who was dark-haired and slender. Both threw their prayer-books high in the air as they sauntered home along the smart suburban avenue where they lived.

Mary walked alone. She was tall, too thin, and mousey. 'A bit of a mess' was her own rather brutal, but true, description of herself. She had not yet learned how to make the best of herself and had not the confidence to try. Enviously she regarded the chic, voluptuous Danielle, as she stepped smartly after the two younger children in her clicking high heels. Mary longed to reach her twenties and attain that self-assurance and control which seemed to her to be the chief prize of adulthood.

Their Victorian town house was just a few yards

away now and Mary could see her father's car parked outside in the road. Dad would be inside, of course, reading the clever people's Sunday papers and quite proud of the fact that he was a *lapsed* Catholic. Mass was for the children; and a religious background, which, of course, he and Mrs Hanrahan also shared, was a sound formative influence. Intelligent, sophisticated adults, however, could dispense with it. It was incompatible with a cultured, mature lifestyle and something to chuckle over at dinner parties.

Mary rather resented this. The fact that she was still sent off to Mass with her sisters and Danielle every Sunday meant that she was still looked upon as a child, and Danielle, and all the other people at Mass would be able to *see* that she was still looked upon as a child. It was embarrassing, like being expected to sit at the table with Meggie or Joanne when they had birthday parties, instead of being asked into the kitchen to help with the food.

As the straggling group of people drew nearer to their destination, however, Mary began to think of something quite different.

She started to feel — she didn't know what — but the only word that she could think of to describe it was — 'dread-full'. Not the usual sort of dreadful which is just another way of saying 'ill' but rather 'full of dread'. She slowed her pace and lagged behind the others, as she tried to work out why she was feeling 'dread-full'. Was it because it was a dull, cloudy day and Mass had been even duller? She shrugged. If that was all it was then there was no need to feel quite so 'dread-full', because most Sundays were dull. Was it because Joanne, 'the baby of the family', as her doting parents called her, had been a pig and a brat all morning? Mary knew that if Joanne continued in her piggishness and bratishness for the rest of the day then she, the oldest sister, would probably be blamed for setting a bad example. No, it wasn't even that. Mary knew that it was a worse thing. Much worse.

Danielle called to her in her soft, lilting accent, 'come on, Mary, you are so slow!'

Mary heard her and sluggishly obeyed, closing the gap between the other three and herself. For some reason, she began to feel that she didn't want to go home. She didn't want to go home because the thing that was making her feel 'dread-full' was to do with home, though she still wasn't sure what it was. She hung her head as she walked along getting left behind again as she re-immersed herself in her thoughts.

Meggie and Joanne skipped and chattered far in front of her, still playing 'catch' with their prayer-books. Whatever the 'dread-full' thing was that awaited them behind the front door, her sisters were obviously unaware of it.

The house loomed larger. As she approached it, Mary's sense of doom increased and began to turn to fear. She was actually *afraid* to go home. She didn't think she could face the unknown, whatever it was that had to be faced.

She didn't know if she could cope with it.

She pictured what lay behind the smartly-painted

façade of the tall, old house, in an attempt to discern the root of her fear.

It was a normal, London maisonette. In the top flat were the Thompsons, an aunt-and-uncle type childless couple, who gave the Hanrahan children sweets and let them feed their tropical fish.

In the bottom flat, the basement, was a single girl who wore black and worked in a theatre. She was out most of the time and had a boyfriend who stayed weekends. She was friendly, even if she was hardly ever in.

The middle flat was the largest and belonged to the Hanrahans. They also owned the front door and the staircase, and they had two floors to themselves. The theatre girl got into her flat via the basement steps, and the Thompsons' front door was off the Hanrahans' bedroom landing.

Of course, Mary knew that in thinking about flats and neighbours she was avoiding thinking about her own home. Her own home, in the sense of the furnishings and fitments, was very pleasant. It was large, light, airy and tastefully decorated, with good wool carpets, art prints on the walls and lots of books. Mr and Mrs Hanrahan were quite comfortably off on their teachers' salaries and could afford the fashionable luxury of a French au pair. Dad was good at finding cheap, junk-shop furniture and doing it up so that it looked really nice. Mum — Mary's feeling of foreboding rose dramatically as she was forced to think of her mother — Mum kept the flat very clean and tidy, and put flowers from the garden in vases.

Mary thought about her mother, her beautiful, attractive, dark and shapely mother.

Danielle called again, 'Mary, what is wrong with you?'

This time there was concern in Danielle's voice. Mary looked closely at her. Did Danielle know what was 'dread-full' at home? Mary knew. Suddenly she knew. From out of the dark haze of her confusion she was beginning to understand. She wished she could go back to not knowing, but of course it was too late.

Chapter 2

What Mary Knew

'Are you all right?' queried Danielle gently as Mary caught up with her. They had arrived at the short flight of stone steps that led up to the Hanrahans' front door. Meggie and Joanne were already at the top of the steps, restless and keen for Danielle to let them indoors.

Mary wondered what she should say to Danielle; whether she should admit that she had discovered the truth, or whether she should play ignorant.

If she played ignorant, she might put off a deeper involvement in the situation for a time, but she realised it would only be for a very short time. In the end, the adults around her would expect her to realise what was going on, because she was thirteen.

If she admitted to knowing the truth now, then everyone would know where they stood, which was less complicated. Yet something deep within her wanted to hold back and pretend. It was the worry that if she confessed to having found out, then the adults would think: Ah. Mary's old enough now to understand all this. Mary can cope with this situation.

Mary didn't think she could cope at all. She felt

she could cope with some adult things, like learning to wear a bra and high heels and putting on mascara, but *this*! Mary was not old enough for this. She was not ready for *this* at all.

Danielle was waiting for an answer. Mary had to say something. There was really only one thing to say, even though Mary did not want to say it, or have it confirmed by Danielle, or have anything more to do with it.

The words left her mouth like a death-wish. 'Mum's not coming back, is she?'

For a moment Danielle was silent, as if she had been expecting this from Mary sooner or later. In the silence, Mary remembered the last time she had seen her mother.

Mum had stood at the front door with Dad. Mary had seen them from the kitchen, but they were not aware of her. Dad was looking imploringly at Mum. He looked shattered and was saying something to her, softly, so that no-one else in the house would hear. Dad was slightly taller than Mum, his hair a greying blond, his face handsome for a man in his forties, but at that moment he seemed suddenly shorter than Mum, old and pathetic.

In contrast, Mum, in her tailored suit and black stilettos, with her dark brown hair tied back in a bun, was tall, erect, decisive and angry.

Of course, Mum was often angry with Dad. That was nothing new. The thing that gave the game away to Mary was not the way she looked, but the suitcases she was holding in her hands.

Mary had retreated from the scene before the

front door slammed and had mentally shelved the disturbing vision until — now.

Danielle was speaking. 'No. I don't think your mother is coming back. You must speak to your father.'

Mary groaned inwardly. This was moving too fast. She didn't *want* to talk about it with her father. She wanted to forget it. She wanted her dinner. That was all she wanted, and to watch 'East Enders'.

They all entered the house, and hung up their coats on the antique coatstand in the tiled hallway.

Danielle said, kindly, 'your father is in the living room. I will take Meggie and Joanne with me into the kitchen, and we will get the dinner ready.'

Danielle must have been aware of the look of fear on Mary's face, for she touched her arm then, and added, 'I am sorry about this, Mary.'

Mary did not respond. Danielle opened the living room door. Unseen, but not unnoticed by Mary, the au pair communicated something, wordlessly, with Dad before departing into the kitchen with the younger girls.

The door was left ajar. Mary entered and sat on an armchair, at a little distance from her father.

He looked as he had done when Mum had walked out: helpless, surrounded by the usual Sunday papers, which today had an unread look about them. Mary guessed that he had just been sitting there all morning, staring into space and being unhappy. He looked so different from the Dad she had known, or thought she had known. She didn't like the way he looked today. It made her feel insecure.

'Well,' he began sadly, 'Danielle tells me you know about your mother.'

Mary nodded. It was odd that he should say 'your mother' like that, when he usually said 'Mum,' or 'Mummy' if it was to the little ones. In future, though, Dad was only ever to say 'your mother', if he referred to her at all.

'I'm afraid she's left us,' he continued. 'She's gone away.'

'Won't we see her again?' asked Mary, panicking.

'Oh, *you* will. At weekends. You can spend Saturdays with her, if you like.'

'Oh.'

Mary tried to come to terms with this. She couldn't. Suddenly, it was a concession to the children that they should see their mother. Didn't children have any say in these things at all?

'It was another man, you know,' continued Dad. 'She had a boyfriend.'

Yuk, thought Mary. I don't want to hear this. This is dirty. This isn't the sort of thing *my* parents ought to be involved in.

Dad continued, relentlessly, and Mary cringed as he spoke.

'I've always loved her, you know. Always. I gave her everything. I'll always love her, but I'll never forgive her for this.'

SHUT UP, thought Mary. I don't want to know.

'Where is she living?' she asked sharply.

'With Brian, of course.'

'In Brian's house?'

'No. They're staying elsewhere. I don't know where.'

'Is she going to marry him?'

'I don't know. She may do, after we're divorced.'

'Divorced!'

'Well, naturally.'

Mary questioned his use of the word 'naturally'.

'What about us?' she asked. 'What about Meggie, Joanne and I?'

'What do you mean?' rejoined Dad.

'Are we going to live with you, or are we going to live with her?'

Dad sighed. 'She didn't want you. I want you. You'll stay with me.'

Mary didn't understand. 'She didn't want us' — what did that mean? She didn't love her children — was that it? It couldn't be. It couldn't be true. It was too cruel. Were their children just a parcel to be thrown back and forth between their parents — 'You have them.' — 'No, you have them.' — was that all they were?

'How could she not want us?' demanded Mary, the hurt making her eyes sting and bringing a lump to her throat. 'She loves us, doesn't she?'

Dad swallowed before replying. His eyes, too, were full of tears.

'I don't know,' he answered. 'I think she wanted Brian more than she wanted you.'

Mary rose to her feet suddenly, and cried freely, sobbing loudly as the full effect of what her father was saying worked within her like a dose of poison. She had no more words.

Her father began pitifully, 'Mary — my dear —' and he held out his arms to her. She backed away in distaste, unable to look at him.

In more pain than she had ever known, she left the room, closing the door.

Chapter 3

Facts of Life

Mary climbed the stairs, half-blinded by her tears and entered the bedroom she shared with Meggie and Jo. She flung herself, face first, on the neat duvet of her own bed and continued to give full vent to her feelings.

After a few moments, predictably, Danielle came in and walked cautiously towards her. Mary knew it was Danielle from the sound of her footsteps and turned round to face her, wiping her eyes with her hand.

'Did you *know*, before it happened, I mean?' she asked the au pair.

'I guessed,' replied Danielle truthfully.

'You didn't say anything,' accused Mary.

Danielle sighed. 'How could I? I am a *servant.*'

Mary was puzzled. She didn't understand how being a servant, if Danielle *was* a servant, made a difference. Danielle's logic went over her head, like everything else.

'Would you like me to leave you alone?' came the accented voice again.

Mary sniffed, nodded and turned her face back to the duvet. There was the sound of retreating high heels and the shutting of the door.

Alone again, Mary sat up and leaned back against her headboard. This bright, cheerful, yellow-and-white bedroom, with its three single beds, became all of a sudden filled with Mary's memories of her mother.

There was Mum, helping Jo to dress in the morning and tickling her. Mum, sitting on Meggie's bed and kissing her goodnight. Mum, alone with Mary just a few weeks ago, coldly handing her that embarrassing book on the facts of life and leaving the room before Mary could ask her any questions.

The facts of life! Mary was beginning to learn a few facts that weren't in that book.

As she sat on her bed, she reviewed her last conversation with Dad, recalling every word and trying to keep up with the pace of change around her.

It was incomprehensible to Mary how her father could send her off to Mass as a child; then after Mass try and share his anguish with her as if she were an adult. Who did he think she was? Did he think she could grow up exactly when he wanted her to? Did he consider her feelings at all, or was he so steeped in self-pity he couldn't see past the end of his own nose?

Things had changed so rapidly. Mary's life had gone into a skid; wild and out of control. She had come home to a different family, to a different father and, so it seemed, to a different Mary.

The bedroom door creaked and in tiptoed Meggie and Jo. They approached Mary's bed and stood beside it, wide-eyed and bewildered.

'What's happening?' queried Meggie, fear in her blue eyes and her plump face pale.

'Hasn't Danielle told you?' rejoined Mary.

'No.' Meggie shook her head. 'We were in the kitchen and Danielle went in to see Dad after she came downstairs from seeing you, so we came upstairs. Why are you crying?'

'Mum's —.' For Jo's sake, Mary paused while she chose her words. 'Mum's sort of — gone.'

'Gone?' repeated Jo anxiously. 'Where's Mummy gone?'

'I don't know. She's with Brian,' answered Mary.

'Why?' responded Meggie innocently, frowning.

Mary was exasperated. 'Look — I can't explain it,' she told them hastily. 'Dad'll tell you. Go and see Dad about it.'

'When's Mummy coming back?' persisted Jo.

Mary felt helpless. Joanne was only four. In many ways, she was really only a baby. How can anyone explain divorce and adultery to a baby? Still less, how could Jo be told her mother had left her and wouldn't be tucking her into bed any more?

'Go and see Dad,' insisted Mary. 'Please.'

The younger sisters shuffled reluctantly out of the room, leaving the door open. Mary heard them go downstairs, Meggie murmuring in reply to Jo's worried demands as they descended. She heard them enter the living room; then she heard Danielle speaking, followed by Dad. Eventually there was the sound of children crying. Mary's heart was breaking for her sisters, now, as well as for herself.

Who was responsible for this? Who had done this

horrible and wicked thing to them? Why should they be treated this way? What had they done wrong? Were they very *bad* children? Were they such awful children that their mother hated them and couldn't bear to live with them any more?

We *aren't*, protested Mary to herself. She *knew* they weren't that bad. It wasn't their fault. They were just ordinary children. Why, then, did Dad say that Mum didn't love them? How could that be true? It was impossible.

Mary remembered Dad's bitterness as he had broken the news to her and she reasoned it out to herself: He hated Mum. He said he loved her, but he hated her. He was trying to turn his children against her, so he lied about her. That was it. Dad must have done something to drive Mum away.

Mary remembered the muffled, unintelligible, 'not in front of the children' rows she had overheard between them in the past few months. They had been ghastly, sick-making rows, unbearable to listen to. Mum's voice had always been the loudest, with Dad trying to pacify her.

No matter, Mary told herself dismissively. It couldn't be as Dad had said. It just couldn't. What about Brian though? There must have been *something* going on. Or was there? Maybe he was just a friend. Mary tried, but was unable to convince herself of this. Okay, so Mum and Brian were in love. Mary and her sisters had been to Brian's bachelor flat with their mother. Mum had told Mary that Brian was helping her with a correspondence course, but Mary had thought at the time that there was something 'funny' going on. That much was probably true, then. But whose *fault* was it all? Mum's, Dad's, or Brian's?

Mary determined to get to the bottom of it; to find out who was really to blame. Dad had said that she could see Mum at weekends. Very well, then, she would and she would make her mother tell the truth. She would find out who was making her sisters cry.

Chapter 4

Dad Makes Some Changes

A fortnight later, and the reduced family were driving through the suburban streets to a different part of London, their father at the wheel of his car. Jo had just completed her first week at the convent primary school which Meggie still attended.

At breakfast that morning, another bombshell had been dropped on the three girls, when Danielle had announced her imminent departure.

'You're leaving?' Mary had repeated, aghast.

'I'm afraid I must,' said Danielle.

'Why?'

'Your father cannot afford to pay me anymore.'

'Oh!' Mary did not understand. 'Why can't he?'

'Because there is only one salary coming in now.'

'Oh, I see.'

And so Danielle had gone upstairs to pack her bags. When the Hanrahans returned from 'wherever-it-was' they were going today, (the children had not yet been told where), the au pair would have left, for good.

Mary regretted this deeply. She had been fond of Danielle and her departure was yet another family upheaval. With the au pair no longer there, Mary presumed Dad would take over the cooking and

17

cleaning and looking after Jo, but still, the prospect
of herself being left the senior female of the house
made Mary feel suddenly rather exposed and nervous.

'I wish Danielle didn't have to go,' she confessed
to her father from the passenger seat of the car.

'So do I,' agreed Meggie vehemently from the
back.

'So do I too,' repeated Jo beside her.

'I know, I know,' Dad said, 'I didn't want her to go
either, but I'm afraid I had no choice.' He paused.
'Still, she was due to leave soon after Joanne started
school, anyway.'

'Yes,' put in Mary, 'but that was before Mum left.
We need her more now than we did before.'

Dad arched an eyebrow.

'What do you mean?' he asked, in a tone that
suggested to Mary she had uttered something offensive.

She hesitated.

'I — I mean it would be nice to have her around
the house, wouldn't it?'

'What for?' queried her father, his eyebrow
arching still further.

Mary wished she had never opened her mouth.

Quickly, she replied, 'I mean — because of the
cooking and the housework and looking after Jo in
the evening, that sort of thing.'

Dad snorted in derision.

'My dear girl,' he told her coldly, 'we hardly need
hired help when there's a teenager in the house.'

Mary swallowed.

'Sorry,' she apologised.

Dad continued, 'you're old enough now to take more responsibility for the running of the household. A girl your age should be quite capable of cleaning and washing and looking after young children.'

Help, thought Mary. Just what am I expected to *do*? With no previous experience of anything more complicated than washing-up, the idea of taking over the role of mother and housekeeper was daunting.

Mr Hanrahan must have noted the look of fright on Mary's face, for he then added more gently, 'naturally, I'll do the cooking.'

'Oh,' nodded Mary, 'thanks.'

'What I propose is this,' he resumed. 'I'll give you a weekly housekeeping allowance of — ' (he named a sum of money) 'and out of it you will buy in the food, pay the milkman, get the newspapers and get things like toilet rolls. Okay?'

'Okay,' responded Mary, trying to commit these instructions to memory. The sum he mentioned may have been generous, or a pittance, for all she knew.

'I'm sure a girl your age can manage that,' he concluded.

Mary was very unsure, but dared not question her father's judgment. She decided to put it out of her mind and changed the subject.

'Has Mum been in touch yet?' she asked tentatively.

Dad winced and looked hurt.

'Your mother has not phoned,' he answered, shortly.

Meggie broke into the conversation from the back seat of the car, 'but you said we could see her at weekends. This is the second weekend and still we haven't seen her.'

'I'm not answerable for your mother's behaviour,' snapped Dad. 'Now, if you don't mind, I'm trying to concentrate on the road.'

Meggie and Mary were silenced. They exchanged a glance, recognising the developing new rule that talk relating to 'their mother' was to be initiated only by Dad, who appeared not to want to contact her.

Jo, catching a drift of the mood of unease, spoke to her father.

'Where are we going?'

Dad relaxed, obviously glad that the conversation could move to a safer topic.

'We're going to see a new house, darling,' he replied.

'A new house!' repeated Meggie in surprise.

'Yes, we're moving out.'

'But why?'

'Our present house is full of too many memories for me. I need a change of scene.'

Mary was disturbed. She *liked* their old house and didn't share her father's concern over 'memories'. It was their home and they belonged there. She looked again at Meggie. From the look on the younger girl's face, the feeling was mutual.

Jo piped up, 'are we going to *live* in a new house?'

'That's right,' Dad answered and leaned conspiratorially towards Mary. 'Of course,' he added, 'there's also the financial question.'

Mary looked blank.

'The *rent*, you idiot,' he explained impatiently. 'We've only got one salary coming in now.'

'Oh!' agreed Mary hurriedly. 'Of course!'

'What's the new house *like*?' asked Meggie curiously.

Dad's answer was vague.

'Oh, you'll see,' he said.

They drove on, and all lapsed into a thoughtful silence. Mary looked out of her window and noticed the change in the townscape around her. The area they had driven into was scruffier than that in which they now lived. The streets were litter-strewn, the houses unkempt, the people shabbily dressed. There were more black and brown faces around than she was used to seeing. Was *this* where they were going to live?

At length, they turned off the main road and began to climb a hill of small, two-storey Victorian terraces. The houses looked mean and cramped. Their front gardens were full of litter and overflowing rubbish bins where thin mongrels rooted for food. The paintwork on the houses was peeling and old, and faded curtains drooped limply behind dirty window-panes.

Dad pulled up outside one of these houses and turned off the car's ignition. 'Well,' he announced in a businesslike, almost cheerful manner, 'here we are.'

There was no response from his children.

Chapter 5

Mary Asks For Help

It was lunchtime at St Columba's Comprehensive, four weeks later, when Mary first told her school-friends what had been happening at home. She, Jill and Clare were sitting on a bench at one end of an asphalted area next to the nuns' neat, pretty garden. Around them, other uniformed girls chatted in the mild April sunshine and, in the garden, three nuns weeded and mowed.

'You've been looking really down,' observed the blonde Jill to Mary. 'That's probably why Miss Wilcox wants to see you.'

'Have I?' said Mary.

'Yes, you have,' agreed the darker Clare, turning to Jill. 'We said ages ago there was something wrong with you. What is it?'

Mary regarded her friends apprehensively. They had been talking about her, and Miss Wilcox, her form teacher, had probably been talking about her too. She was going to have to 'go public' despite her desire to keep her increasingly sordid home life to herself. How would Jill and Clare react to it? Both of them came from secure, middle class backgrounds comparable to what her own used to be. Having to tell her friends about the parental split was bad enough, especially since they were Catholics, for whom divorce has added stigma, but added to that was the downmarket house move. What would they think?

'Tell us what's wrong,' urged Clare, concern evident in her brown eyes. 'We're your friends.'

Mary sighed. Yes, they were indeed her friends, so she would have to tell them.

'It's my Mum and Dad . . .,' she began and related the story up to the point of the house move.

Their reaction was the obvious one and it did not help Mary. Jill and Clare were very shocked and pitied her. From that moment, she felt that pity had opened up a chasm between herself and her friends, and between herself and the rest of the world. She wasn't the same as everyone else anymore. She was unfortunate, marked and separate; someone for whom people were 'sorry'. It made her feel isolated and estranged from 'normal' people.

'You must feel *awful*,' Clare told her sympathetically when Mary had finished her tale. 'You poor *thing*. It must be really horrible.'

'It's just terrible,' added Jill. 'Fancy not having a Mum around anymore. I just couldn't bear it. I really need my Mum. Poor Mary . . .'

Mary was torn between wanting to run away and the feeling that she *ought* to cry. She imagined Jill and Clare would expect her to cry, but Mary did not want to reinforce their image of her as the suffering semi-orphan. What she wanted them to do was forget the whole story, since they couldn't really understand how she felt. Also, she wanted them to treat her like an ordinary person again, so she pretended she didn't really care about it at all.

'I'll survive,' she told her friends, with a careless shrug. 'It's not the end of the world.'

At that point Miss Wilcox, a well-built woman in her early thirties, walked up to the bench. She was attractive rather than pretty, with short, light brown hair and grey eyes. She wore a fawn skirt suit and flat shoes.

'Are you ready?' she enquired gently.

Mary could detect the sympathy already.

Clare and Jill withdrew as Miss Wilcox led Mary off the asphalt and into the nuns' garden. The teacher and pupil talked stiltedly about schoolwork until they reached the most secluded part of the garden, where the grotto stood. They sat down together on a green-painted bench, Miss Wilcox adopting a relaxed posture, Mary bolt upright.

Opposite them was the grotto itself, a high rockery with its central statue of Our Lady, arms welcoming, as St Bernadette had seen her. At the base of the grotto was a small pond, to represent the healing waters of Lourdes, and all around were carefully tended roses and little bushes. It was the 'holy' part of the nuns' garden and Mary was very privileged to be allowed in.

'I often pray to the Virgin Mary, in times of trouble,' commented Miss Wilcox.

Mary refused to respond to the hint and fixed her eyes, instead, on the statue.

Our Lady had such a sad, loving, gentle face and her long garments were a pale sky-blue. Our Lady understood everything perfectly and required no awkward explanations. Presumably God and Jesus understood as well.

Miss Wilcox broke the silence.

'Your father has told us all the details, of course. It's a tragic thing to happen to a family, and Joanne only four years old, poor little mite.'

Still Mary said nothing, her gaze on the statue.

'Your father told us you've moved house. Do you like your new house?'

'It's okay,' answered Mary reluctantly. 'I don't mind it.'

In reality it was far from 'okay', but she wasn't going to tell Miss Wilcox about the dirt and smells of her new environment, or about how small the house was. Neither would she tell her how much she missed the car, now that it had been sold, or the washing machine that had also gone. Then there was the outside toilet, the black, damp mould that covered the kitchen walls and the mice that scuttled about the floor at night. She would not talk about that, because it would make Miss Wilcox feel even more sorry for her.

'What are your neighbours like?' asked the teacher after another long pause.

Mary could tell Miss Wilcox was finding the conversation difficult and she felt guilty for being so unco-operative, but she still wouldn't, or couldn't, give her what she wanted.

'I haven't spoken to the neighbours, much,' she replied truthfully. 'There are some Pakistanis on one side, but the parents don't speak English and the kids are still in nappies.'

'What about the other side?'

'Oh,' answered Mary vaguely, 'there's a woman and two girls about my age. They're white. I think one of the girls is called Susan. They seem okay, but they've gone on holiday or something.'

'Oh well,' said Miss Wilcox. 'You might become friendly with them when they get back. That would be nice, wouldn't it?'

'Mmm.'

The teacher drew in her breath, evidently realising that the small talk was achieving little.

'You must miss your mother,' she suggested.

What sort of a question is that thought Mary and said nothing.

Miss Wilcox tried again. 'I'm sure she'll be in touch soon.'

Mary's eyes left the statue for the first time and she looked at her would-be confidante.

'Did Dad say where she was?' she asked, with interest.

'No. I'm sorry. He doesn't know.'

'Oh.'

A heavy silence descended once more, broken eventually by the bell announcing the start of the afternoon's lessons. Miss Wilcox stood up.

'Well,' she said softly to her pupil, 'if you ever need to talk, you know where to find me. Please don't hesitate. I *do* understand how hard it must be for you.'

No you don't, thought Mary. She looked up at Miss Wilcox.

'Do you mind if I stay here?' she asked hesitantly. 'I'd like to pray for a minute, to Our Lady.'

'Of course,' smiled the teacher. 'Take your time.'

When she had disappeared out of sight and there was no sound but the rustling of leaves and the song of birds, Mary dropped to her knees on the grass and crossed herself.

'Holy Mother of God,' she prayed. 'Help me. Please help me. I want my Mum back.'

Chapter 6

'The Prince of Wales'

On the Saturday morning of that same week, it was
Mary's turn to go to the laundrette. She and Meggie
had, by now, worked out a rota for all the domestic
chores, doing things alternately between them. Dad
and Jo did not contribute, apart from the occasional
evening meal or lunch that he prepared.

Doing the laundry was the major Saturday job,
apart from giving the house its weekly clean and
tidy, a task also reserved for that day. So, while
Meggie hoovered and wiped, it fell to Mary to haul
the bulging plastic carrier bag of dirty washing
down the hill to the corner laundrette.

It was a sunny, fresh, spring day and a few, brave,
golden daffodils bloomed in the tiny, front gardens
of the terraced houses. A cool breeze blew in from
the Thames, and Mary was contemplating a solitary
afternoon trip on the Woolwich free ferry, when
Susan drew alongside her.

'Hi!' the girl called happily. 'Are you going down
the laundrette?'

'Yes,' answered Mary.

Susan struck her as being quite a shy person,
who, for some reason, was putting herself out to be
friendly. She was probably a local, to judge from the

broadness of the accent and Mary guessed she must be approaching fourteen. She did not dress like the other local girls, who, in Mary's opinion, wore their clothes too tight, their heels too high and showed too much leg and bust. Local girls smoked, but Susan didn't. Her face was plain and she had a brace on her teeth. Her hair was mousey, like Mary's, and she was as plump as Mary was thin. Her eyes were her most interesting feature; not that they were large or of an unusual colour, but they seemed to radiate a cheerfulness and warmth which Mary found appealing. She felt that Susan might be nice to know.

'Do you want a hand?' offered the local girl. 'The bag looks heavy.'

'Yes please,' replied Mary, and they took a handle each.

They continued down the hill, the bag of dirty clothes between them. Mary again got the feeling that Susan was fighting hard to overcome her shyness. This had the effect, oddly, of putting Mary at her ease.

She asked Susan conversationally, 'where did you go for your holidays?'

'Oh, to my Auntie's, in Billericay. That's in Essex.'

'It's not far to go for a holiday.'

'It's all Mum can afford. Have you got a Mum?'

Mary paused before replying, 'she's dead.'

'Oh, I'm sorry,' said Susan, her smile fading. 'My Dad's dead.'

Mary was taken aback by this. She had lied about her mother in order not to have to talk about her.

She wondered whether Susan had done the same regarding her father.

'He died in a car accident,' the other girl explained. 'Jenny and I — that's my younger sister — we were only little, so we don't really remember him. Has your Mum been dead long?'

'No.'

'How did she die?'

Mary was stumped for a ready answer.

'She — um — died of cancer,' she said at last.

'Oh,' nodded Susan. 'That's bad. What does your Dad do?'

'He's a teacher.'

'My Mum's a nurse.'

There was a pause.

'It's a shame for Jo,' remarked Susan. 'She's a bit little not to have a Mum.'

Everyone feels sorriest for Jo, thought Mary resentfully.

'She cries a lot, doesn't she?' continued Susan. 'We can hear her through the wall.'

Mary pulled a face.

'She's a pain in the neck,' she said. 'She always used to be spoilt, 'cos she's the youngest, but now Mum's gone she's even worse. She gets really naughty, 'cos she misses Mum, and Dad expects *me* to sort her out, presumably 'cos he can't cope with her himself, though how he reckons *I* can cope beats me. *I* can't handle her. Every time she plays up *I* get the blame. *I* hate her,' she concluded with feeling.

'Do you?' responded Susan.

'*Yes.*'

'Don't you have any aunties and uncles to help out?'

'No. All Dad's family are in Ireland and Mum's are in the North; not that Dad has anything to do with them.'

'Why won't he have anything to do with them?'

'Oh —.' Mary had come unstuck again. She couldn't tell Susan it was because he thought they were hiding Mum; not now she had said Mum was dead.

'They just don't get on,' she told Susan instead. It was true, really.

'That's a shame. We've only got an aunt in Billericay, but Mum managed okay when Dad died, 'cos people in the church helped her. Do you go to church?'

'Yes, I do.'

'What sort of church?'

'Catholic. St Patrick's, down the road.'

'Don't they help out?'

Mary was puzzled at the concept of total strangers rallying round. Even where they had lived before, the other church-goers were only really acquaintances.

She answered, 'no, they don't. But they don't know me at St Pat's, because we're new to the area. Anyway, I'm the only one who goes now. Dad never went, neither did Mum and now he isn't bothered whether we go or not, though he used to be.'

'So you go on your own?' asked Susan.

'Yes, I like going.'

'Do you? Why?'

'Why is she so interested in talking about churches?' Mary asked herself. 'People don't normally
talk about religion like that.'

'I don't really know why I go,' she answered
honestly, glad that Susan obviously didn't think it
peculiar to go to church. 'I used not to like it, when I
was *made* to go, but now that it's my own choice, I
kind of enjoy it. Maybe it's just that I'm so used to
going it'd seem funny to stop.'

'I see. Do you think it's just a habit then?'

Mary thought about it.

'No,' she said carefully. 'It's not just that. It's sort
of — peaceful — there, and I can be on my own,
nice and quiet for a change, away from Jo and the
house. Also I like to pray about things. I need to get
away from home so that I can sort of — build my
strength up.'

'Build your strength up for what?'

Mary shrugged, realising she was giving too
much of herself away.

'Oh, just — things,' she told Susan. 'Jo — and —
things.'

'It sounds as if it's hard at home.'

'It is.'

They had arrived outside the laundrette. Mary
looked in at the rows of washing machines and
driers, all in use, and the regular launderers with
their many baskets of wet washing.

'Looks busy,' commented Susan.

'It always is on a Saturday morning.'

'Oh well, I'll be off, then.'

'Yeah, okay. Thanks for the hand with the laundry bag.'

'Anytime. See ya.'

With a smile and a wave, Susan was gone. Mary entered the warm, steamy laundrette and began the long process of doing the weekly wash. As she sat watching the clothes go round and round in the machine, she thought about Susan, hoping they would become friendly enough for Mary to be able to trust her with the truth regarding her mother and other things that were going on at home, like —.

Mary's heart sank. Through the glass frontage of the laundrette she watched her father walk quickly down the busy street and enter the 'Prince of Wales'. She looked at her watch. She knew she wouldn't see him again for hours on end.

Chapter 7

Breaking Point

At one o'clock that afternoon, Mary shoved open the front door and dumped the heavy bag of still-damp laundry onto the floor of the narrow hallway.

'Meggie!' she called aloud. 'Give us a hand with this lot!'

There was no response, so Mary tutted and made her way through to the tiny kitchen at the back of the house, from which wafted an appetising smell of hot food. Meggie and Jo were there, in front of the greasy cooker, Meggie having just shut the oven door.

'This casserole's going *black*,' Meggie complained to her older sister, 'and Jo keeps whingeing 'cos she's hungry.'

'Oh no. Did Dad say we weren't to eat it 'til he got back?' asked Mary wearily.

'Yeah,' answered Meggie with an equally weary nod of the head. 'He said he'd be back in half an hour and that was two and a half hours ago.'

'Not *again*.'

Jo grizzled, 'I'm starving. I want something to eat.'

'Well you can't,' Meggie remonstrated irritably. 'He'll kill us if we start without him, like he did last time.'

Mary sighed. 'This is ridiculous. Every time he cooks he does this now. He did it three times last week. How does he expect us to go without food for hours and hours?'

'I don't know,' commiserated her sister. 'You know, of course, he won't be home 'til much later in the afternoon.'

'That'll be hours, by the time he rolls home,' added Mary.

'I want my dinner,' wailed Jo again.

'Oh, shut up,' rejoined Mary. 'You're not the only one that's hungry. I'm starving too.'

'And me,' put in Meggie. 'Is there any bread?'

Mary went to the grubby larder cupboard opposite the cooker and looked in. There wasn't very much there: some instant coffee, a few tea bags, tinned beans and spaghetti, margarine, cereal and — yes — half a loaf of white sliced.

'We can have this,' she said, giving them a slice each. 'I'll get some more later, when I go shopping.'

Meggie snorted in derision as she chewed her bread.

'You, shopping? That's a joke! I can't remember the last time I had cake, or biscuits, or proper meat.'

'That's 'cos I can't afford them,' snapped Mary, to whom this issue was becoming increasingly sensitive. 'He doesn't give me enough. By the time I've paid the milkman and the laundrette on a Saturday there's hardly anything left for food.'

'Dad says Mum used to manage on what he gives you.'

'Look!' shouted Mary in sudden fury. 'I haven't

got enough money! I do my best to make it last, but it just *doesn't*, that's all!'

Meggie continued mercilessly, her spite sharpened by hunger.

'He says you spend it all on biscuits and hide them and eat them yourself and don't give us any.'

Mary's anger rose even higher at this injustice.

'That's not fair! It's a lie and it's stupid! I don't do that, not ever! He's making it up! He's only saying it 'cos he knows he doesn't give me enough! *You* should try it! *You* should try making the money last! *I* can't do it and I don't see why I should have to! *I* have to do *everything* round here, *everything*! It's not fair!'

With that she swept out of the kitchen, through to the shabby dining room with its dusty dresser and sticky table and chairs.

'Did you tidy up in here?' she demanded, in an angry voice, back to her sister.

'Yes I did,' came the tetchy reply.

'Well it doesn't look like you've touched it!'

Mary progressed quickly to the front living room. The threadbare carpet had been hoovered and the top of the black-and-white TV dusted, but apart from that it did not look any different from the morning. Mary picked up a cushion from the sagging settee. Beneath it was a collection of sweet-papers and magazines. On the untidy bookcase stood the same half-cup of cold coffee that Dad had placed there the night before.

'You've done *nothing* in here!' yelled Mary, her voice trembling with rage. 'You haven't tidied it at *all*!'

Livid, she marched back to the filthy kitchen, where Meggie and Jo still stood, picking at slices of dry bread.

'Do it again!' she demanded imperiously.

'I've done it,' grumbled Meggie. 'I'm not doing it again.'

'But you haven't done it!' shrieked Mary in protest. 'Not properly! You haven't even wiped down the dining table, or cleared the rubbish out of the front room, or dusted the shelves!'

'They don't need doing.'

'They do! This place is like a pigsty!'

Meggie shrugged her shoulders insolently.

'No-one's bothered about it except for you. If you're so bothered about it, why don't *you* do it?'

'Because it's *your* job!' screamed Mary.

'Who says? Only you!'

'Dad told me to see the house was clean!'

'Dad says you're a bully.'

Mary gasped in horror.

'Have you been moaning to him about me?'

'Yeah, why not?' sneered Meggie. 'You're always bossing us around. Dad says you should do it all yourself.'

'Does he?'

'Yeah.'

At this, Mary let out a cry of frustration and rage, and flew at her sister in a spontaneous and vicious attack of violence, scratching with her nails and pulling Meggie's blonde hair. Her sister fought back with equal belligerence, kicking, biting and pinching. They fell to the dirty floor together in a frenzy of aggression, their bodies crashing and colliding into fridge, cooker and cupboard.

'I hate you!'

'I hate you!'

They hissed, screeched and swore at each other; wrestling and struggling until they were both exhausted and weeping. Finally, they pulled apart, their anger dissipated and their shared emotion, now one of abject misery and hopelessness.

Jo's voice came above the sound of their crying. In a self-righteous, smug tone she declared, 'I'm telling Daddy on you two. You're *naughty*.'

Together, Mary and Meggie turned to look at her, stifled their sobbing and glared threateningly.

'Don't you *dare*,' Meggie snarled, her voice low with menace. 'You disgusting little *sneak*.'

Jo was shocked into silence.

Chapter 8

After-dinner Conversation

It was long past three when Dad's key was heard rattling at the door. His children were in the front room, watching TV, and they listened carefully to his attempts to gain entrance, having learned to gauge his degree of drunkenness by the amount of difficulty he had in getting his key into the lock.

'Only half sloshed,' observed Meggie. 'He must be short of cash.'

'I hope he goes straight to bed,' said Mary.

Half sloshed was worse than fully sloshed. If Mr Hanrahan was fully sloshed his habit was to stumble about downstairs for a while, then crawl up the stairs to bed, where he would quickly fall into a snoring slumber. If he was only half sloshed, on the other hand, he usually picked a fight with either, or both, of the older girls first and only then go to bed, demanding a cup of tea to be brought up after him.

Unfortunately for his daughters, however, Mr Hanrahan was only half sloshed this afternoon, as Meggie had accurately predicted.

As he walked into the front room his older daughters exchanged a look of anguish. Mary quickly vacated the settee to go and sit on the floor by Meggie's armchair. This was a precaution against the possibility of Dad sitting beside her. Jo was cross-legged in front of the TV, with her back to them. She turned round as her father appeared.

'Daddy!' she greeted him, with relief, as she got to her feet.

Mr Hanrahan slumped down heavily on the settee and his youngest snuggled up close to him. He put his arm around her, as a stale odour of beer and cigarette smoke filled the room.

'Daddy,' Jo told him innocently. 'The cass'role went all horrible. We could only eat *some* bits.'

Mary groaned inwardly. Brilliant, she thought. 'We can always rely on darling Jo to let the cat out of the bag.'

Half an hour ago, Mary and Meggie had, by mutual agreement based upon extreme hunger, shared out the still edible parts of the casserole, throwing the burnt and dried-out residue away and swearing Jo to secrecy. They had hoped Dad would forget about the meal and he might well have done so, if Jo had kept her mouth shut. Now, however, there would be a row. Mary could feel it brewing, as Dad's eyes narrowed and he scrutinised her with suspicion.

In a voice expressive of both incredulity and hatred he said, 'you *ate* it?'

Mary tensed up. She was afraid of her father's temper, especially his drunken temper, which was verging on the psychotic.

'It wouldn't keep any longer,' she explained apologetically. 'We didn't know when you'd be home.'

'But I told you to *wait*. I said not to eat 'til I came home!'

'But you said you'd be home in half an hour!'

'I was delayed.'

'By *five hours*?'

Mary overstepped the mark at this point. She knew her father was spoiling for a fight and she had, stupidly, taken the bait.

'The length of time I'm out,' insisted Mr Hanrahan, slurred and irate, 'is no concern of yours. I told you to wait for me and *that alone* is your concern.'

'But Jo was hungry!' protested Mary, knowing all the while that he did not want to listen to reason.

'Bah!' scoffed her father. 'I'm sure Joanne was perfectly all right, weren't you, my love?'

These last few words were directed with gentleness at the youngest girl, whose answer was a compliant and predictable, 'yes'.

'There, you see!' said Mr Hanrahan, vindicated. 'Don't you try and make an excuse out of Jo! You were just greedy — too greedy to wait for me!'

'But Meggie was hungry too.'

'I was, Dad,' put in Meggie timidly.

'Nonsense,' he resumed. '*She* put you up to it. She's greedy! Greedy!'

Mary struggled to make him see sense.

'But if we'd left it any longer it would have been uneatable anyway!'

'Rubbish! Rubbish! All you had to do was turn the gas down — that was all!'

'But it was already down on the lowest gas!'

'It was not.'

'Yes it was!'

'No it wasn't!'

'It *was*!'

'Are you calling me a liar?' challenged Mr Hanrahan.

Mary braced herself, mustering all her courage to defy him.

'Yes,' she said.

There was an awful silence and the three girls seemed almost to stop breathing. Mr Hanrahan rose to his feet, tottered slightly and shook his head very slowly at his eldest child.

'That does it,' he told her bitterly, sounding unnaturally calm as he managed to suppress his fury. 'You've had your chips with me, my dear. You're no sort of a daughter for a man. People say to me: "How lucky you are, Mr Hanrahan, with a grown girl to look after you and the little ones" and I have to tell them: "No. She's no good to me at all. She steals food from their mouths and bullies them. She's useless." You're a wicked, greedy, selfish, stupid, thoroughly nasty piece of work. Just like your mother. Yes, *exactly* like your mother.'

By the time he finished this speech, Mary was shaking with fear, anger and grief, and tears were flowing down her cheeks. Mr Hanrahan left the room, slamming the door behind him.

The children heard him climb the stairs, open his bedroom door, close it, and heave his body onto his bed. When all was quiet, they relaxed and Meggie went to Mary's side. The older girl was crying silently and still trembling with emotion.

'He's awful,' Meggie consoled her sister. 'I hate him too.'

From upstairs came a shouted demand: 'Meggie! Fetch me up a cup of tea!'

Chapter 9

Mary's First Protestants

The Sunday morning was breezy and bright, much as the day before had been. Mary, who had her own room now, was up at ten. She dressed herself hastily for Mass, bemoaning the fact that she had nothing to protect her bare legs from the chill wind.

Her wardrobe was, in fact, becoming a source of concern to her, as it was some time since her mother had last kitted her out. She was starting to fill out widthways and shirt buttons kept popping. It was useless sewing them back on again. She had managed to purchase a bra out of her pocket money, but only one, which was often, subsequently, put on still damp from washing, or, if it was really wet, not at all.

Her hips had also broadened, so that her trousers and jeans looked so tight, now, as to be immodest. That left the skirts, which still fitted, but the trouble with wearing skirts so early in the year was that tights were really a necessity and Mary could not afford to buy more than one pair a month. Her current pair were full of holes, therefore unusable.

She put on her one pair of shoes and went downstairs.

Meggie and Jo were still in their bedroom, so she

had her father's early morning presence all to herself. He was in the kitchen, making himself a cup of coffee. As Mary entered, she attempted a cheerful greeting.

'Morning!'

No response.

'Any hot water left in the kettle?'

Silence.

Mary's worst suspicions were then confirmed. She had half-expected this after yesterday. Coventry was Dad's preferred method of punishment these days. It could go on for over a week and it was agonising.

'I'm going to Mass this morning,' she announced, for the sake of something to break the silence.

Dad grunted his disapproval.

Mary tried hard to maintain her illusion of joy.

'Do you want me to get lunch today?' she suggested helpfully. Surely this must provoke a reply.

It did not.

She made herself a mug of coffee and poured out a bowl of the cereal she had bought the previous afternoon. That reminded her: 'Dad?' she queried tentatively. 'Can I have my housekeeping money for next week?'

'You may not,' he answered curtly, without looking at her.

It really speaks, thought Mary. The answer, however, was disconcerting.

'What do you mean?' she asked.

'I mean you may *not*,' came the short reply. Dad still would not look at her.

'Why?'

'The other two have given me bad reports about you. You obviously cannot be trusted with the money. You spend it all on yourself. In future, *I* shall have to do it.'

'Oh.'

Mary could not find it in her heart to object. She was relieved to have the burden removed from her shoulders. Obviously, though, she would remain in disgrace.

Dad walked swiftly past her, out of the kitchen, through the adjacent dining room and into the front room. The TV went on and the volume was turned up.

As Mary worriedly ate her breakfast, she wondered how long her Coventry would last this time. Each time it happened, it seemed to go on for longer, and her pocket money would be stopped, all of which had a very depressing effect. The ghastly silence was always so heavy and so laden with unstated loathing that it gave her headaches and made her feel permanently on edge. It was a subtle and effective form of torture and her father knew it. She was doubly glad now that it was time to go to Mass.

Anything to get out of the oppressive house. *Anything* to get away from the dreadful, suffocating atmosphere. *Anything* to get away from *him*.

Hastily, she went into the hallway and donned her coat, opening the front door onto sunshine and fresh air.

Next door, Susan, her younger sister Jenny and

their mother were also leaving their house. The two front doors were separated by the thickness of a single wall, so greetings were unavoidable.

'Hi,' said Mary, who was not in the mood for conversation. She walked down the short path to the gate, but was forced to halt in her tracks by the sound of Susan's mother's voice.

'Hello Mary,' said Mrs Fellowes, with a smile. She was a slim, chirpy redhead of about forty and she had a soft Scots accent. 'Do you want a lift to St Pat's?'

'A lift?'

'Yes.'

Mrs Fellowes waved to a car parked in the street outside. It had its engine running and a sandy-haired young man was at the wheel. She explained: 'Neil usually comes and picks us up to take us to church. St Pat's is on our way. It'll save your legs. My name's Jean, by the way.'

Mary hesitated, unsure of whether to accept the offer.

'Well, if it's no trouble,' she said uncertainly.

'Of course not,' Jean reassured her, as they all stepped onto the pavement and closed their respective gates.

Neil opened his car doors from the inside and Susan's mother bent down to speak to him.

'Room for one more as far as St Pat's?' she asked.

'Sure,' agreed Neil. 'Hop in.'

Mrs Fellowes sat down in the passenger seat beside him and the three girls clambered into the back, Mary between Susan and Jenny. The younger girl had red hair, like her mother, and looked to be about eleven.

Soon, after Jean had introduced Mary to Neil, they were driving down the quiet Sunday High Street. Mary was listening to the chat of the other passengers, who talked about mutual friends and 'meetings'; whatever *they* were.

Mary got the impression from their conversation that everyone in their church knew each other and did a lot of activities together, the precise nature of which eluded her. These activities, 'The Prayer Group', 'The Outreach', and 'The Bible Class', had a distinctly 'Protestant' ring to them, unlike the more familiar Legion of Mary or Knights of St Columba, at St Patrick's and Mary deduced that the Fellowes must, indeed, be Protestants.

Like a lot of convent-educated, Catholic, Londoners, she had never got to know any Protestants before in her brief life and regarded them as something of a curiosity. In fact, up until the time she left primary school, she had believed England to be a Catholic country, with Protestants as a heretic minority.

Susan broke into her thoughts.

'We go to Gladstone Street Baptist Church,' she said, as if in answer to a question.

'Oh, I know it,' nodded Mary. 'It's only a few streets away from St Pat's.'

'Yes, that's right.'

Neil looked over his shoulder at her from the driver's seat.

'Are you a schoolfriend of Susan's?' he enquired in a friendly manner.

'Oh — no — no. I go to St Columba's.'

'Ah yes, of course. I hear it's a good school.'

'I go to Erith Green Comprehensive,' Susan told her.

'Do you?' asked Mary, who associated Erith Green with glue-sniffing and teenage pregnancies, in accordance with its popular reputation.

The expression on her face must have given her thoughts away, for Susan reassured her: 'It's not as bad as people say. Only a few people do the vandalism and stuff. In fact, it's got a big CU.'

Mary was puzzled.

'A what?'

'A Christian Union.'

'What's that?'

Neil interrupted.

'I don't think Mary will have come across that,' he explained to Susan. 'Catholic schools don't tend to have them.' He added, for Mary's benefit, 'it's a group of people who meet regularly for prayer and worship.'

'I see,' said Mary, really none the wiser. Prayer and worship? It sounded a bit fanatical.

'Here we are,' Neil said, as he pulled up near the brick-built Catholic church.

'Thanks.'

Mary exchanged goodbyes with the others in the car and watched as they drove away. A sudden gust of wind brought up the goose-pimples on her bare legs. She turned and walked, alone, up the street to St Patrick's.

Chapter 10

Food and Cash

There was a knock at the Hanrahans' door at five o'clock, just five minutes after Mary reached such a height of boredom and restlessness that she had decided to go to evening Mass.

It was a worse-than-typical Sunday evening — not much on the telly and even less in the larder, for Mr Hanrahan, despite his vow to take over the housekeeping from yesterday on, had still not been to the shops.

'Someone's at the door,' observed Meggie from behind the Sunday Times.

All three girls were in the front room at the time, lounging about on the furniture and drinking tea to stave off hunger-pangs.

'Someone had better answer it then,' remarked Mary, drily in response, her eyes remaining fixed on the TV.

'You do it,' countered Meggie.

'No, you. I did it last time.'

'That was on Thursday, when the milkman came for his money!' retorted Meggie indignantly.

'So?'

'Well, you've had time enough to recover.'

'That's beside the point.'

'What *is* the point?'

The knocking was heard again. Mary got up with an exasperated sigh.

'You're ugly, *that's* the point,' was her parting shot as she left the room. She opened the front door on Mrs Fellowes, who was smiling rather nervously.

'Yes?' Mary enquired.

'I wonder if you girls and your father would like to come to tea this evening,' began Jean. 'Our guests have had to let us down at the last minute and it seems a waste, all that baking, if there's only us three to eat it. We were going to ask you for next week, anyway. Of course, if you've already pre-pared your tea . . .'

Mary found the thought of 'preparing' a bowl of cornflakes rather funny.

'Er — well, I'll have to ask Dad,' she told her neighbour, surprised at the sudden invitation. 'He's asleep — I think.'

'Sure,' agreed Mrs Fellowes. 'Give us a knock and let us know when you've spoken to him. See you in a few minutes, then.'

'Okay, thanks,' said Mary as Jean retreated. She closed the door and went back into the front room.

'Sue's mother's asked Dad and us to tea,' she told her sisters.

'To tea?' repeated Meggie.

'Yeah,' grinned Mary. 'You know — food.'

'Food!' Meggie's eyes widened in anticipation.

'She said she's *baked*. That means *cakes*.'

'Wow! I'm going then.'

'Me too,' said Jo, eager for the feast.

'We've got to ask Dad, though,' Mary reminded them sombrely. 'And I wouldn't put it past him to say "no" just to spite us, the mood he's been in lately.'

Meggie's face fell.

'Rats,' she grumbled, 'he's still out for the count upstairs. He's probably not even sobered up yet from lunchtime. I don't reckon he'd want to go anyway.'

'Quite,' muttered Mary. 'If he's still tight we don't even *want* him to go. He'd just embarrass us to death.' She brightened. 'We could go on our own, of course. Without him.'

'Without asking him?' questioned Meggie doubtfully.

Mary considered it. 'No, better not. *You* ask him, though. He's still not talking to me.'

Meggie nodded.

'Okay,' she agreed. 'If I don't shake him too much and I ask him while he's still half-asleep then he might say "yes" without thinking about it.'

'Hope so,' said Mary. 'Come on then. I'll go up with you to see what he says.'

'And me!' put in Jo.

'No,' Mary told her. 'You stay down here, out of the way.'

Jo whined pitifully.

'Go on,' she pleaded.

'No!' snapped her sisters together.

Subdued, the younger one fell into a sulk while Mary and Meggie closed the door on her as they made their way, quietly, upstairs.

'Remember — don't shake him too much,' advised Mary in a whisper, 'and if he just sort of grunts then we'll take it as a "yes".'

'Okay.'

The two conspirators arrived at their father's bedroom door. From within his untidy den, with its piles of old newspapers, dirty, crumpled clothes and empty whisky bottles there came the sound of deep snoring and a faint whiff of the pub.

'He's well away,' remarked Mary. 'Go on.'

Meggie carefully opened the door and tiptoed in, while Mary stayed in the doorway, out of sight, watching.

Their father lay like a tramp on the bed he had shared with Mum. He was fully clothed and sprawled above the covers. On his bedside table lay a pile of loose change, the turn-out from his trouser pockets. It struck Mary, not for the first time, that he looked like a rather revolting, old man and not the kind, paternal creature she had grown up with. She had lost all respect for him.

Meggie shook his shoulder gently.

'Dad,' she said in a low voice.

He mumbled in his sleep.

'Dad,' repeated Meggie as she shook him again.

He stirred, like a giant, out of his slumber.

'Urr?' he mumbled, opening his eyes drunkenly.

'Dad?' asked Meggie. 'Can we go next door for tea?'

'Uh?' came the sleepy response.

'Next door for tea.'

He made an irritated snorting sound and turned over.

'Do what you like,' was his disinterested answer. Meggie looked round at Mary, smirked and gave her the thumbs-up sign. Mary returned it with a smile and Meggie and she left the room, shutting the door.

'That wasn't so bad!' commented Meggie.

'Yeah. This means we can *eat*.'

'You'd better go next door and tell Jean.'

'Mmm ...'

Mary had just had a new idea, a very daring, sinful and criminal idea and she was busy mulling it over in her mind.

'Aren't you coming down?' queried Meggie from the top of the stairs. 'You've got to go next door.'

'Yeah,' answered Mary in a far-away voice. 'Come here a minute.'

Curiously, Meggie returned to her side.

'He's still asleep, right?' began Mary, softly.

'Yes?'

'And he didn't wake when you went in,' she continued.

'No.'

'Have you noticed how he always takes the loose change out of his pockets and puts it on his bedside table before he goes to bed?'

Meggie nodded.

'I bet I could go in, steal some, come out, and he'd never even notice.'

Shocked, Meggie breathed, '*steal* some? You wouldn't dare! Would you?'

'I need some tights,' explained her sister. 'He's not even talking to me and he won't give me any pocket money. Stealing is the only way I'm going to get a penny out of him.'

'But supposing he woke up while you were doing it?'

Mary shrugged.

'I bet he wouldn't.'

'He'd *murder* you,' objected her sister.

Mary tutted.

'It's only an idea,' she said, starting to go down the stairs. 'I didn't say I'd actually *do* it, did I?'

Chapter 11

False Impressions

'I don't like Mary Hanrahan,' remarked Susan as she rejoined her mother in their clean, bright, red-and-white kitchen.

'Don't you?' said Jean.

'No. I don't.'

The Hanrahan girls had just departed the house after finishing their tea and Mrs Fellowes was washing up. Susan picked up a tea towel from the back of a pine chair and started to dry plates, putting the finished ones onto the worktop in front of her.

'She seems such a misery,' she went on, with a frown.

'I'd say she was unhappy,' corrected her mother.

'No,' Susan disagreed, 'she doesn't come over as unhappy, as such. Just sort of stand-offish and unfriendly.'

'Those might just be the symptoms of her unhappiness.'

Susan shrugged dismissively. 'Well, all I know is she sat there with a face like a wet weekend and hardly said a word. She kept looking daggers at her sisters and all her sisters were doing were talking and eating. Boy, did they eat, but Mary hardly touched a thing. *And* she's a liar.'

56

'A liar?'

'Well, she told me her mother was dead and she isn't dead at all, 'cos Meggie told us she's left home.'

Jean sighed and shook her head.

'Susie,' she explained patiently, 'you've only absorbed one half of what was going on. How do you think Mary must have felt when Meggie blew her cover about their Mum?'

'A bit stupid, I expect.'

'Exactly. Up to the point when Meggie did that, Mary had been quite cheerful and tucking into her tea. When Meggie started telling us about life next door, however, Mary stopped eating and that's when she clammed up and started to look miserable, glaring at her sisters.'

Susan was puzzled.

'But *why*?'

Jean smiled.

'There's a saying — "even the poor have their pride". Mary has her own dignity to preserve and that of her sisters. She doesn't want everyone to know their father's a drunkard, or that their mother walked out on them, or that they're badly treated, poor and ill-fed.'

'Ill-fed?'

'Look at the way their eyes lit up when they saw the tea-table! The way Meggie and Jo ate, I reckon it was their first proper meal all day.'

'Yes,' Susan said thoughtfully. 'Poor things. How awful.'

'Which is the sort of reaction Mary was trying to avoid by not telling the truth. When people have got

big problems like that and other people find out
about it, the problems can suddenly become the
most important thing about that person, with the
person themselves becoming secondary.'

'Eh?' Susan did not understand.

'Well, let me put it this way. Mary is afraid we'll
think of her as the girl with the alcoholic father, or
the girl from the broken home and nothing more. I
felt a bit like that when your father died. I felt I'd
been labelled "The Widow", and it wasn't a good
feeling.'

'But *we* wouldn't label her like that, would we?'

'We *shall* not. But maybe other people have.'

'I see.'

Jean poured the dirty water out of the bowl and
refilled it to clean the glasses.

She continued pensively.

'Mary is a proud girl, from a proud family. She
stopped eating because she didn't want to be on the
receiving end of our charity.'

'Our charity!' repeated Susan, shocked. 'We
weren't giving *charity*!'

'Of course we weren't,' reassured her mother,
'but Mary's very sensitive about it, probably because the family aren't *used* to being poor and *she*
will see it as charity.'

'She's very touchy.'

'So might you be, in her situation.'

There was a pause, as Jean washed the glasses,
and Susan wiped them. Eventually Susan spoke.

'She must be very unhappy, then. She usually
looks tense.'

Jean nodded.

'Yes, I've noticed. But we've all heard the rows that go on in that house through the walls and we've seen Mr Hanrahan roll home from the pub night after night. It's enough to make anyone tense.'

'Then why aren't Meggie and Jo as miserable as Mary?'

Jean washed a tumbler slowly, as she considered her answer.

'I'm sure Meggie and Jo are suffering,' she said at last, 'but Mary is the oldest child and there may be pressures on her that aren't on the younger ones. Apart from that, she's at an awkward age,' (Susan was embarrassed at this last reference) 'and her father doesn't seem very fond of her at the moment.'

'How do you know?'

'Oh, well, we've exchanged the odd word. It was an impression I got.'

'That's really tough,' sympathised Susan. 'She must be so unhappy.'

'Yes,' agreed Jean sadly, 'yet I'm sure if she had something to be happy about, you'd see a quite *different* Mary.'

'What — you mean if her Dad stopped drinking so much, or if her Mum came back?'

'Well, yes, that would make a big difference, of course, but we can't bank on either of those things happening.'

'So she's not likely to stop being miserable then.'

'No . . ,' said Jean, musingly, 'but you're forgetting

something. There's something else that could cheer her up.'

'What?'

'Oh, really, Susie, I shouldn't have to tell you *that*.'

Susan was mystified, then after a few moments, the penny dropped.

Chapter 12

Good Catholics

The next time Mary and Susan encountered one another was the following Friday, as Mary was taking a walk. It was a cool evening and a golden sun was descending low over the Thames. Mary reached the hill-crest of Backmount Road, where she lived, and noticed Susan walking towards her. Mary felt immediately uncomfortable, because of Sunday's tea-time disclosures, but Susan gave no sign of remembering them.

'Hi,' she greeted Mary, her grin revealing the brace on her teeth.

'Hello,' returned Mary.

'Going for a walk?'

'Yes, I am.'

'It's nice out.'

'Yes.'

There was an awkward pause, then Susan seemed to collect herself and said, 'listen, I was thinking on Sunday, and I was going to ask you. It's just — um.' She hesitated. 'Mum wondered if you'd like to visit our church one Sunday. You see — the reason is — there's a Sunday School for Jo and a Bible Class for Meggie; that's instead of the Lord's

Table and the sermon. Mum thought they might enjoy it, 'cos St Pat's doesn't have those things, does it? We wondered if you'd like to come along, too.'

'Oh!' Mary was taken aback slightly, but didn't mind being asked. 'Well — um — I don't know. I can ask Meggie and Jo, but really I'd have to ask Dad about it, or rather, they would.'

'Oh yes,' said Susan, a note of relief in her voice. 'Of course you would.'

'They might like to go,' Mary added encouragingly.

'Great,' smiled Susan. 'What about you?'

'Me?'

Mary had mixed feelings about this idea. On the one hand, she was growing to trust and like the Fellowes, because they were nice to the Hanrahans, but on the other hand, she was a Catholic and tried to be devout.

'I'm not sure,' she told Susan honestly. 'I mean, in a way I'd like to go, but you're Protestants, aren't you?'

'Yes,' agreed Susan, looking concerned. 'I suppose we are.'

'Well, you see,' continued Mary, trying to soften the blow, 'we're not supposed to take communion with you; at least, that's what I've been taught, so I don't know if I ought to go, really. I'm sorry,' she concluded, meaning it. 'I mean, it's nice of you to ask.'

'Oh.'

Susan, obviously disappointed, then said, 'but you don't have to take communion.'

'No, I know,' responded Mary thoughtfully, 'but I

still don't think it'd be right for me to go, when I should be at Mass, 'cos it's a sin to miss Mass.'

'I didn't realise that,' Susan said. 'I understand. I mean — I understand your position.'

'But I'll definitely ask for Meggie and Jo,' Mary said reassuringly. 'It's different for them, you see, 'cos they wouldn't be in the service, so they wouldn't have to worry about not taking communion, if you see what I mean and anyway they don't go to Mass, so they can't "miss" it any more than they do already.'

'Okay,' said Susan. 'Thanks for passing the message on, anyway.'

'I'll let you know the answer,' concluded Mary. The two girls parted company with a friendly 'goodbye'.

The opportunity to broach the subject of the invitation to Dad came after school the next day, though Mary had told her sisters about it the day before. Both were keen to accept and were determined to twist their father's arm, should he prove obstructive. Mr Hanrahan was still not talking to Mary, so she was unable to speak on Meggie and Jo's behalf.

'Dad,' wheedled Meggie as they were eating their tea of beans on toast. They ate in the living room these days, in front of the TV and with their plates on their laps.

'Dad,' she began, 'can we go to Susan's church on Sunday?'

'What?' rejoined Mr Hanrahan, with a frown, though it was obvious he had heard.

Meggie repeated herself and he shook his head decisively.

'They're not Catholics,' he said, as if that were the final word.

'But they're *nice*,' reasoned Meggie.

'*Nice*?' repeated Dad with scorn. 'They're Bible-bashers and God-botherers, that family; that's what they are.'

'Oh, Dad,' said Meggie reprovingly.

'We're not having anything to do with religious maniacs,' insisted their father. 'Not only are they Protestants, though I admit some Protestants are perfectly civilised and I've got on very well with them; not only are they *that*, but they're evangelical, a sect with which any self-respecting *Anglican* would want nothing to do, let alone a *Catholic*.'

Mary, whose blood had been slowly coming to the boil throughout this discourse, could refrain from speaking no longer.

'Since when have you been such a *Catholic*!' she scoffed. 'It's years since you even set *foot* inside a church! Who are you to pass judgment on other people!'

Dad glared at her angrily.

'I'm a good Catholic,' he told her, 'born and bred and I shall die a Catholic. It's in the blood, and it will always be so.'

'Then why do you make fun of me going to Mass?'

Her father laughed cruelly.

'You have the faith of a peasant,' he informed her.

'Stupid!' shouted Mary, setting free the feelings she had been bottling up against him for nearly a week. 'If you're such a good Catholic, then why are you getting divorced and why don't you go to Mass and why do you drink so much?'

Dad roared at her.

'How dare you talk to your father like that! After everything I've done for you! I could have had you put into care with the Social Services after your mother "upped and left", but out of the goodness of my heart I didn't and this is the thanks I get! How dare you!'

'But you're my father! It's your duty to look after us! Why should I have to be grateful to you? It was you and Mum that got us into this mess, not your children!'

Meggie interrupted.

'Look, aren't we getting off the point? We were supposed to be talking about the Fellowes —'

'They're no Fellowes of mine,' quipped Mr Hanrahan humourlessly.

'I think you're being unfair,' went on Mary, who was a glutton for punishment. 'The Fellowes are okay — so what if they're Protestants? They're our friends!'

'I have my own friends,' Dad rejoined loftily.

'Oh yeah?' sneered Mary. 'And where have your posh friends been these past few weeks, eh?'

'Get out!' barked her father. 'Get out of my sight, you insolent, cheeky, evil creature! Go to your room!'

'Glad to,' snapped Mary rudely, flouncing out.

An hour or so later, when Dad had gone out to the pub and peace reigned once more in the troubled home, Meggie came upstairs to visit her sister in her bedroom. Mary had, by then, stopped crying and had calmed down.

'Guess what,' Meggie announced gleefully.

'What?' asked Mary absently. She was nursing a guilt complex for her bad behaviour.

'He says we can go!'

'You can go?'

'Yes! He gave in! We managed to persuade him before he went out. Well, it was Jo really, with her poor little baby act.'

Mary managed a chuckle.

'Good old Jo. So she has her uses, after all.'

'Right,' agreed Meggie. 'You didn't do *yourself* any favours, though.'

Mary pulled a face.

'I haven't got much left to lose,' she replied.

Chapter 13

Sally and Sarah's Helpful Hint

The following morning was a dull, cloudy Saturday. Mary resolved to try and 'make the peace' with her father. There were two reasons for this decision: in the first place, she was plagued by her conscience, knowing that she had insulted him and, secondly, she was still desperately short of cash.

She knew she had a bad temper and a short fuse, and she regretted it, almost frightening herself at times by her own lack of self-control. She was genuinely remorseful for her last outburst and determined to make amends and apologise as soon as possible.

The problem with 'waving the white flag' at Dad was that he tended to use admissions of guilt as grist to his mill. He would take as long as he wanted to bestow forgiveness, leaving the repentant sinner in an excruciating state of anticipation and longing for several days before he eventually climbed down. This was to be one such occasion.

Mary had rehearsed her lines, having taken advice from the 'agony' page of an old teenage magazine.

Sally and Sarah, the 'agony aunts', advised

reasoning with parents, giving them full and honest explanations and offering unreserved apologies. Sally and Sarah also suggested expressions of affection for the parent/s, such as, quote: 'Just telling Mum/Dad "I love you".'

Mary had her doubts about the possible effect of this last gesture, but was prepared to try it if all else failed. After all, it was true. She loathed, despised and hated him, but he was still her father and she still loved him. She wished she did not love him, because then she would not care about the things he said and did that hurt her, but love him she did.

He was sitting at the dining room table, correcting a pile of homework and wearing the reading glasses that made him look particularly stern. Mary entered the room from the kitchen, carrying with her two steaming mugs of coffee. One of these she placed on the table in front of him and the other she clutched nervously in her hands as she stood on the other side of the table from him.

'Dad?' she ventured meekly.

Predictably, he gave no sign of having heard.

'Dad,' she began again, 'I've made you a coffee.' Silence.

'Dad, can I talk to you?'

'What?'

He looked up from his work, peering at her through his lenses as if she were a naughty child in the headmaster's office.

'Dad,' Mary continued tremulously, 'I'm sorry — about the things I said yesterday. I didn't mean them.'

'Didn't you?' he rejoined coolly. 'I'm not so sure.'

As a matter of fact, Mary still *meant* every word. She was just sorry she meant it.

'I am sorry, really,' she said nevertheless. 'Please say you forgive me.'

Dad looked back down at his papers and gave a disbelieving half-laugh to himself. He carried on marking homework.

Time passed.

'Please say you forgive me, Dad,' repeated Mary.

No response.

'I really am sorry. Really I am.'

Nothing.

'Please Dad,' went on Mary, a note of desperation entering her voice. 'I can't stand it when you don't speak to me.'

More silence.

'Dad, please,' she begged. 'Please speak to me.'

He did not.

'Dad, *please*. I hate it when you won't talk.'

Evidently her father quite enjoyed the experience.

'Dad —,' Mary paused, hesitated, then flung caution to the winds. 'Dad — I *do* love you!'

At this, Mr Hanrahan looked up sharply, an amused, sardonic expression on his face.

'I *beg* your pardon?' he queried.

'I love you, Dad,' she said worriedly, realising all the while that the ploy had not worked.

He laughed in her face and blasphemed scornfully.

'Dad — don't laugh at me,' pleaded Mary.

He ignored her request, muttering as he carried on writing.

'Never heard anything like it. Never in all my born days. Idiot child. What a ridiculous thing to say.'

Mary sighed helplessly and her tears started to drop down into her coffee cup. She left the room and went upstairs.

Chapter 14

Father Moloney Advises

In the afternoon, she went to confession at St Patrick's.

The confessional boxes were like large double cupboards of dark oak, set into the red-brick side wall of the nave, and they had signs above the doors. There were two sets of two, one set for each of the priests in attendance and you had to 'queue' in the pew at right angles to the box of your preferred confessor, until your turn came to go in.

Mary liked Father Moloney the best. He was young, gentle and Irish. She seated herself to wait outside the door with his name above it. When he was ready to hear the next penitent, a green light would show above the penitent's door of the confessional and when the box was occupied, the light would turn to red. There were three penitents ahead of Mary, all middle-aged and all three must have been terrible sinners, for Mary had to wait over half an hour before the green light signalled her to go in.

She left her place in the pew, opened the carved door of the confessional, went in and closed it behind her. The dimly-lit box was just big enough for one person to sit down in and was panelled in dark wood, a tiny stained-glass window set in the far wall. Inside the box was a prie-dieu and she knelt down on it, joining her hands to pray after she had crossed herself.

Father Moloney was sitting in a similar box next door to Mary. The two were separated by a wooden wall, into which was set a mesh grille, behind which, on Father Moloney's side, hung a thick, red curtain. The purpose of the grille and curtain was to prevent the ready identification of the penitent, whilst still permitting the confession to be heard.

Mary listened as Father Moloney pronounced the blessing in a low, quick, almost inaudible voice and she prepared to make her confession.

'Bless me, Father, for I have sinned. It is six weeks since my last confession.'

'Go on, my child,' came the soft, confidential voice of her confessor.

Mary then told him everything — not just about her sins of temper and hatred, but about her anxiety and loneliness, too.

When she had finished, Father Moloney said soothingly, 'well, my dear, it's very hard growing up, to be sure. I'm very sorry about your mother, such a shame. Maybe your father will settle down in a while and not drink so much, when he's got used to the new domestic situation.

You know, it must be very hard for him, very hard indeed. Maybe he gets a little impatient and a little preoccupied with himself and all the difficulties. What I advise you to do is just try and bear with it a little longer and try to see *his* point of view. I know it's hard, but try and count to ten every time you feel angry and you'll be surprised how well that works. Meanwhile, I shall remember you in my own prayers. When you feel lonely, remember Our Lord was lonely too, in the Garden of Gethsemane. He knows how you feel. You could try doing voluntary work, perhaps with the elderly. People very often make new friends that way and, you know, it helps to take you out of yourself when you realise there are other people worse off. Does that help?' the priest concluded hopefully.

'Yes, Father,' whispered Mary, greatly comforted.

'Good,' sighed Father Moloney. 'Now, for your penance, say for me two Hail Marys, and a Glory Be, after I've pronounced the absolution.'

'Yes, Father.'

Father Moloney recited the prayer conferring God's forgiveness for her sins and he said goodbye.

'Goodbye, Father,' whispered Mary and left the confessional box with a much lighter heart.

Just *telling* the priest had helped her. It had really eased the burden and Mary resolved to try and be better, now that she had a clean slate. She wasn't sure whether she wanted to work with the elderly, but at least it was a positive suggestion. She always felt really *good* after confession, as if all her sins had been washed away and she was pure again, pleasing to God. She knelt down in an empty pew and crossed herself, preparing to pay the spiritual penalty for her sins. Two Hail Marys and a Glory Be was about average. She assumed a murderer would have to go through the entire Rosary at least a dozen times.

Chapter 15

Dad Asks a Favour

Meggie and Jo went to church with the Fellowes the next day, while Mary went to Mass. When she returned, Dad was out. Susan and her sisters were in the Hanrahans' front room, drinking tea. Mary was surprised to see Susan there: none of the Hanrahan girls had dared invite their schoolfriends to the depressingly, seedy house. Susan, however, appeared not to mind the untidiness and dirt.

'Hello, Mary,' she said with a smile.

'Oh. Hello Susan.'

Mary sat down on the settee.

'Mum's getting dinner,' Susan explained. 'Meggie said I could come round for a bit, 'til Mum calls me.'

'Oh.' Mary turned to Meggie. 'Did you enjoy Gladstone Street?'

'Yeah, we did,' enthused her sister.

Mary could tell she was not just saying this to be polite.

'I went to Sunday School,' announced Jo proudly.

'What was it like?' Mary enquired.

'Nice.'

Jo looked happier than she had for a long time.

'We had stories,' she continued brightly, 'and singing, but I didn't know the songs.'

'She means the choruses,' Susan told Mary. 'They were probably new to her.'

'Choruses?' queried Mary.

'They're just sort of — short songs.'

'Never heard of them,' remarked Mary, pulling a face to express indifference.

'Meggie went to Bible Class,' Susan went on.

'Yeah?'

'It was really good,' volunteered Meggie, with a nod. 'I liked it.'

'Really.'

To tell the truth, Mary was astonished at this display of obvious appreciation from her sisters, since they were not naturally 'churchy' children. She had expected them to be bored stiff. Also, she was a little jealous, since they appeared to have had a better time at Gladstone Street than she had had at Mass.

'You ought to go along too,' suggested Meggie, as if reading her thoughts. 'It's a lot more friendly than St Pat's.'

'I don't think so,' said Mary half-heartedly.

'Are you sure? It wouldn't hurt just the once,' remarked Susan, who seemed to want Mary to go.

'I don't know. I wouldn't mind going, I suppose, but I don't know what Father Moloney would think about it.'

'Why don't you ask him?'

'Perhaps.'

'Well, you're welcome at our church anytime.'

Mary acknowledged the offer with a nod, as a knock was heard at the door.

'That'll be Mum,' Susan said, getting up. 'I'll be off then. See ya.'

'Yeah. Bye,' said the Hanrahans and Susan went home to her roast dinner.

The Hanrahan girls dined on toast and margarine, followed by half a packet of digestives between them. Meggie and Mary were in the kitchen after this meal, making cups of tea, when their father returned, unusually early and unusually sober. He went into the front room first, where Jo was still eating biscuits, then, shortly afterwards, joined his older daughters. He seemed ill at ease.

'Girls, may I have a word with you?' he asked.

This behaviour was not normal. Something was up, obviously. He had said 'girls' too, using the plural, so he must have meant to include Mary.

She looked at him wonderingly and somewhat suspiciously.

'I mean you, also,' he added to her.

She dared not say, 'so you're talking to me, then.'

That was not the way things were done. When Dad ended a Coventry, to comment upon the fact would be to risk an immediate reimposition. So she had to pretend there had never been a Coventry in the first place.

Mary and Meggie exchanged a curious glance, as their father pottered about making himself a cup of tea. There was not so much as a sniff of alcohol about him: highly irregular.

'A friend of mine is coming to visit us next week,' he explained diffidently.

'A friend?' repeated Mary, trying to get into the mode of speaking to him again.

'Yes, a good friend,' her father went on. 'Someone I work with — a teacher, divorcée. A highly educated lady —'

Lady!

Meggie and Mary looked at each other, shocked and horrified. Dad had a girlfriend! Oh *no*!

' — very intelligent and cultured,' he continued. 'I want us to make a good impression on her, so I need you two girls to really clean this place up and make it look decent.'

'When's she coming?' asked Mary, wide-eyed.

'On Wednesday,' answered Dad, having difficulty meeting her gaze. His attitude was guarded, his smile uncertain, as if he needed her support.

'I want you to be on your best behaviour,' he instructed his daughters. 'You must make her feel welcome. I'd like to think that my relationship with Deborah had a future, so naturally you three would form a part of that future. Deborah could be an excellent mother for you, so I'm sure you won't let me down.'

The two sisters stood aghast as their father took his cup of tea out into the front room. When he was out of earshot, Mary gasped, her grey eyes expressing her stunned disbelief.

'A *mother*!' she exclaimed in a voice barely above a whisper.

'A *mother* for *us*!' repeated Meggie in similar tones. 'What a *cheek*!'

'We've *got* a mother!' continued Mary vehemently. 'Does he seriously think we're going to instantly regard some girlfriend he's picked up somewhere as a substitute mother!'

'What a nerve! Who does he think we *are*?'

'I want *my* Mum,' insisted Mary, 'not someone I've never even *met* before!'

'Too right,' agreed Meggie, with feeling. 'He can get knotted if he thinks I'm going to suck up to *her*!'

'*And* me,' echoed Mary emphatically. 'Bloomin' *cheek* of it. He can get lost! I wondered why he was talking to me all of a sudden — now I know!'

'Yeah — he only decided to be nice 'cos he *wanted* something.'

'Bloomin' nerve. "Deborah"!' mocked Mary. '"Deborah" indeed. No *way*. No *way* are we going to play *that* game. Oooh, if only we could get in touch with Mum. Our real Mum, our proper, only Mum.'

'There must be something we can do about it,' said Meggie anxiously. 'There *must* be a way we can reach her.'

'I only wish I knew how, though,' Mary said pensively. 'I mean, we haven't seen her now for weeks. We can't *make* her get in touch; we haven't even got a 'phone number, or an address. Suppose she doesn't know we've moved? Maybe that's why we haven't heard from her. I miss her so much,' she concluded, yearning suddenly.

'Me too,' sighed Meggie, equally wistful. 'What can we do, though? Dad refuses to let us look for her.'

They stood, thinking, for several moments. Then Mary said, 'there must be something of hers about the place — letters, with addresses on them. Maybe they could give us a lead.'

Meggie brightened as she suddenly remembered:

'She had diaries — and address books! She left them behind — in Dad's room — I'm sure she did! I'm sure I've seen them in Dad's room!'

Chapter 16

Victory

Deborah's cause was lost before she entered the house, so prejudiced were Mr Hanrahan's eldest children against her.

She was in her early forties, fairly slim and dark-complexioned, with black eyebrows that met in the middle and straight, very dark hair, tied back. She dressed 'arty', looked intellectual and the toenails of her bare, sandalled feet were painted scarlet.

Mary took an instant dislike to Deborah's toenails, as she did to the rest of Deborah.

She and Meggie had done as they were told and had, between them, managed to make the house look cleaner and tidier than it had since they moved in. All this had been done under the close observation of their father, of course, who had even *helped*, so keen was he to make a favourable impression on the new woman in his life.

Thus, as the Hanrahans and Deborah sat in the front room taking afternoon tea and sandwiches, the setting was perfect for purposeful socializing. Perfect, that is, except for the presence of the two 'saboteurs' and their destructive 'stratagem'.

At first, Deborah was at ease and relaxed. Under ordinary circumstances, Mary and Meggie might even have liked her. She had greeted the children in an amiable, uncondescending way and tried to converse with the older two on equal terms. Mr Hanrahan copied Deborah's pleasant manner and, after the two adults had exchanged a few words together about their school, the encounter proceeded as follows:

'How do you like your school, Mary?' Deborah asked politely.

Mary grimaced.

''S all right,' she muttered.

'What's your form teacher like?'

'All right.'

'How do you find the work? Hard, I expect,' suggested Deborah, with a nervous smile.

'It's okay.'

Nonplussed, Deborah glanced at Mr Hanrahan, read his expression of irritation and turned her attention to Meggie.

'Are you looking forward to going to St Columba's next year?' she asked in an interested tone of voice.

'I'm not bothered,' answered Meggie, without looking at her.

'It's a big step, changing schools.'

Meggie obviously considered this a statement rather than a question and did not feel obliged to reply.

There was a brief pause, then Dad spoke up, agitatedly looking from his children to Deborah.

'Meggie is a little shy with strangers,' he told his girlfriend by way of apology.

'Of course. That's only natural,' laughed Deborah unconvincingly, her attention reverting to his eldest daughter. 'What are your favourite subjects at school, Mary?'

'English and History.'

'Oh, really? Those are my best subjects, too. Which period of history is your favourite?'

'Um — Tudors, I suppose.'

'Oh, yes,' smiled Deborah, beginning to relax again. 'Henry the Eighth is such an interesting character, don't you think?'

Mary nodded, looking away as she did so.

'And the Reformation —,' continued Deborah, floundering once more. 'I find that interesting too, don't you?'

'Yes.'

There was another uncomfortable pause, then Mr Hanrahan said, in a strained voice, 'Mary reads a lot of books, don't you, dear?'

Dear?

She realised, with a certain satisfaction, that the plan was working.

'Yes,' was her abrupt reply as she gazed down at the carpet.

'Do *you* read much?' said Deborah to Meggie.

'No.'

In something approaching desperation, the interloper turned to Jo.

'I expect you *love* books, don't you?'

'Yes.'

A slightly more lively interlude ensued, between Jo, Dad and Deborah, but even Jo had got the general drift of her sisters' mood and the possibilities of this conversation were soon exhausted.

Deborah tried to talk to Mary and Meggie about pop music, but she evidently did not know a great deal about current trends and the girls were not prepared to supplement her knowledge, so this topic too, died a death.

Long before this point, however, Dad had grown annoyed, at first, and then angry at his children's behaviour and was struggling hard to restrain himself from chastising them. He was studiously well-mannered as he addressed them, his eyes steel-grey and narrow, his smile fixed and false, like a mask. He continually made excuses to Deborah for his children's sulkiness, talking to her of convalescence from tummy bugs and general shyness.

Mary, however, was carefully observing Deborah's reactions to the things Dad was saying and knew that the woman was not fooled. She was not reassured by his reasoning and she recognised the fact that she was beaten. Her demeanour became subdued, where once it had been outgoing and the smile had disappeared from her face.

Mary knew that she and Meggie had won and that Dad and Deborah had lost, but it was a hollow victory and one that gave her no joy. She felt rather sorry for the woman and knew that their treatment of her had been cruel and unfair. She wanted, now, to explain to Deborah *why* they had acted as they did, but of course this was not possible.

The whole incident left her feeling empty and sour inside; not triumphant, as she had anticipated, but once more guilty and once more hating herself.

Deborah departed early in the evening.

After Dad had seen her to the door, he returned to the front room and his children. Meggie and Mary received the blasting for which they had been mentally prepared and which they accepted, almost as a penance. Disgustedly, their father conveyed to them his bitter disappointment and outrage, declaring Meggie and Mary to have ruined his, and their, chances of happiness in a second marriage.

In vain did Mary plead that if Deborah was really keen on the relationship she would not be put off so easily. Dad insisted on viewing the prospect of a new family to have been utterly spoilt, forever. Whichever of them was correct, Deborah never returned.

Chapter 17

Mrs Hanrahan's Secrets

The children breathed a grateful sigh of relief when their father eventually stomped out of the house for his evening visit to the pub, but the prevailing mood was solemn and gloomy as the girls watched TV and ate their tea.

'I feel rotten,' admitted Mary as she finished her meal of cheese on toast.

'Me too,' agreed Meggie, still eating. 'Still, he's only got himself to blame. He *made* us hate her.'

Mary shrugged.

'Yes and no. It was *us* that stonewalled her and it was *our* choice. I feel a bit sorry for the poor woman.'

'Well *I* don't,' declared Meggie self-righteously.

There was a pause, as the two girls thought their quite separate thoughts.

'One thing meeting Deborah did do,' said Mary at last, 'was that it made me realise how much our Mum is *our Mum*, if you see what I mean.'

'Eh?'

'What I mean is — it made me realise that we'll only ever have *one* mother and that anyone else is just — another woman. I knew it before, but somehow actually *seeing* this "other woman" made it come home to me even more strongly.'

Meggie nodded, with understanding.

'I see what you mean, now. Yes, I think that too. Shall we go up, then, for the diaries or whatever?'

'Yeah.'

The girls put their tea-plates down on the floor and, according to their pre-arranged plan, made their way upstairs to their father's messy bedroom. Due to their father's presence in the house during the 'tidying up for Deborah' purge, this was the first opportunity they had had to carry out their investigations, since they conceived the idea.

With Jo tugging along behind, eager for the adventure, they opened the bedroom door, surveying the smelly, littered chamber, dim and dingy, with its half-drawn curtains.

They lowered their voices as they entered, as if he were within earshot and not half a mile away. Sneaking into his den while he was out of the house was a bit like robbing the Pharoah's tomb — illegal and all the more exciting for being so.

'The wardrobe,' announced Mary and she opened it, scanning the contents: suits on hangers, shirts, shoes, bags, hats even, but no papers, no diaries. Nothing of Mum's.

'Try the bedside table,' she suggested next.

The bedside table revealed balled-up socks, underpants and carelessly-folded jumpers, but still no clues.

'Where can he have put her stuff?' wondered Meggie. 'I'm sure it's *somewhere* in this room.'

'The dressing table,' said Mary.

Together, Meggie and she rooted in the little

drawers of this last piece of furniture. It had four drawers, two either side of the central mirror: one side for Mum and the other side for Dad. Naturally, they began their search on their mother's side.

She had left behind some old, used-up cosmetics, some jewellery trinkets, sunglasses, perfume bottles and, most importantly, a collection of half-a-dozen pocket diaries. It was odd that she should have left these behind her when she left. Maybe she had simply forgotten to pack them.

Mary removed the diaries from the drawer with breathless anticipation and threw them onto the bed as if they were buried treasure.

'Got them!' Meggie and she cried together and they picked them up in awe, flicking through the tiny pages and reading the words greedily. Even Jo picked up a diary and copied her sisters' behaviour.

'There's addresses here!' Mary told Meggie.

'And in this one!'

'Writing in here, too,' added Jo, not knowing what was going on.

The sisters reclined on their father's bed and spent the next half hour or so going through the entries in their mother's diaries; except for Jo, who soon decided she preferred to play with the old make-up. It was not the addresses, however, which they found the most interesting, but the daily notes, certain of which were highly significant in the eyes of her daughters.

As long ago as five years, were the entries:

'Went to Brian's.'

'Brian came round.'

'Met Brian for lunch to discuss work.'

And there was another odd comment, made in the same year:

'Have discovered I'm five months pregnant.'

This obviously related to Jo. So, Mum didn't find out she was expecting until she was five months gone? To Mary, this was an indication that the baby was not planned. Poor Jo. She wasn't even an afterthought. After such an unfortunate start to her life, things had not really improved for her. They seemed, in fact, to be on a downward spiral.

As Mary read on, references to their father's drinking started to appear:

'Richard out again tonight.'

'Drunk again.'

'Richard failed to turn up on time — usual reason.'

'Drunk, so forced to cancel restaurant table.'

All this was quite a revelation to Mary, who had assumed her father only started drinking heavily after Mum had left home. Mary wondered why she had not been aware of his alcohol problem while the household was still intact. Had Mum hidden the situation from her children? Had she and Danielle formed a protective buffer between him and his daughters?

It gave her a strange feeling, reading her mother's private thoughts. It was like a glimpse through a curtain at a mysterious, dark world, where alien beings dwelt. The diaries, rather than bringing the truth into the light of day, seemed to tell her: This is adult business. You don't know the half of what went on.

The secrets, truths and lies of the Hanrahans' marriage were not to be discovered within the pages of these small books; they were, in reality, safely locked inside the memories of her parents. Would Mary ever be able to find out *exactly* what had gone wrong and *exactly* who was to blame? She did not feel she could trust her father's word on the matter. Surely her mother would not withhold the facts, if only she could talk to her.

The girls startled suddenly as a knock was heard at the door. Meggie and Mary shot a glance of fear at each other.

'Who's that?' gasped Meggie.

'How should I know?' responded her sister. 'Quick, put the diaries back. We can come and copy down the addresses some other time.'

Hurriedly, they tossed the books back inside the drawer, shut it and rearranged the room to look as if they had not intruded. Then they left it, closing the door and went downstairs. Meggie and Jo re-entered the front room, leaving Mary to answer the door.

The person standing outside it was Susan.

Chapter 18

Conspiracy

'Oh, it's only you,' sighed Mary, with relief.

Susan regarded her with mock-haughty surprise.

'Terribly sorry,' she rejoined. 'Who were you expecting, Princess Di?'

'Sorry, I didn't mean it like that. Come in.'

As Susan entered and joined Meggie and Jo in the front room, she observed, accurately, 'you lot look guilty. Like you've just been up to something.'

Mary and Meggie glanced at each other, wondering whether to take Susan into their confidence. Mary made the decision.

'It's about our Mum . . .,' she began and told Susan the story so far.

'So you're going to try and trace her through those addresses?' she enquired when Mary had finished her tale.

'Yes.'

Susan started to bite her thumbnail thoughtfully and was about to say something, when another knock was heard.

'Oh, that'll be Jenny,' she explained.

Meggie and Jenny had become quite good friends and Jenny was to become a frequent visitor to the Hanrahan house.

Meggie and Jo went to answer the door and when Jenny entered, all three went upstairs to the younger girls' bedroom, leaving Mary and Susan alone.

'Yes, as I was saying,' continued Mary after the interruption, 'it may take some time to track her down, but we've got to do it.'

Susan remained pensive.

'I see,' she said. 'Why isn't your Dad in on this, though?'

'*Him*? Oh no,' replied Mary decisively. 'Whenever we've told him how much we want to get in touch with Mum he just brushes it off. He doesn't want us to try and reach her, so we've got to go it alone.'

'I see,' said Susan. 'But your Dad wouldn't like what you're doing, would he? I mean, you're doing this behind his back.'

Mary expressed her indifference.

'That's just too bad. She's *our* mother. We've got a *right* to see her if we want to.'

'Mmmm ...'

'Well,' demanded Mary, distressed at Susan's evident disapproval, 'haven't we?'

'Yes ... Yes, I know you have. It just seems a bit —.' She hesitated.

'A bit what?'

'A bit underhand, that's all.'

There was a tense pause.

'I know it's underhand,' admitted Mary finally. 'But we've got no choice but to do it this way, unless we want to let our own mother slip through our fingers.'

Susan nodded.

'You're in a difficult position,' she conceded sympathetically. 'I don't know what I'd do if I were you.'

'You'd probably do what we're doing.'

'I suppose I might.'

A thoughtful silence fell again, as a happy sound of girlish chatter drifted down from the bedroom above.

At last, Susan asked, 'if you find her, what will you say?'

Mary had not given this a great deal of thought, at least, not in detail. She knew what she wanted to know, but she did not know how best to find it out.

'Er . . . well, I suppose I'd ask to speak to her . . . and then . . . I'd ask her why she had just abandoned us.'

'What else?'

'I expect I'd ask her why she left Dad — and us.'

'What do you think the answer's going to be?'

Mary pulled a face.

'Dunno. Probably she'll say it's because the marriage went wrong, or because of Brian, or Dad drinking.'

'That doesn't explain why she left you children, though. She could have taken you with her.'

Yes, Susan was right. The last question was the most difficult. Mary could not imagine why Mum had chosen to abandon her children. The only explanation she could think of — that Mum didn't really care for them — was much too hard to swallow.

'There has to be a really good reason,' Mary insisted. 'There must be some really vital *reason* why she didn't take us. That's why I've got to ask her, to find out, 'cos I can't work out this *reason*.'

'But suppose —.' Susan stopped herself. 'No, forget it.'

'Forget what?'

'Oh ... nothing.' She sought to change the subject. 'Have you been to see Father Moloney, like you told me you would?'

'Oh, yes,' replied Mary, remembering. 'I went to see him the other evening.'

'What did he say?'

Mary smiled, her mood lifting as her thoughts were taken away from her mother.

'I was really surprised. I thought he'd say no, but he didn't.'

'Didn't he?' asked Susan, equally bewildered.

'*No*. He said, strictly speaking, I shouldn't, but he didn't see the harm in just a single visit, provided I go to Mass in the evening to make up for it and provided I don't take communion with your people.'

Susan looked appreciative.

'That's not bad,' she commented.

'No. So I think I'll come with you on Sunday, just the once.'

'Great!'

Mary became preoccupied again.

'Listen,' she told Susan, 'I've got to go upstairs to copy down those addresses, so I can get to work on them as soon as possible. Do you mind if I leave you?'

'Oh, okay,' said Susan, getting up. 'I ought to go and do some homework, anyway.'

Mary rose also.

'You won't tell your Mum, will you?' she asked anxiously as they went to the door. 'You won't tell her what I'm doing, will you?'

Susan looked uneasy and seemed not to know how to reply. After some inner struggle, however, she answered: 'No. Okay, I won't tell.'

'Thanks,' said Mary gratefully.

When Susan had departed, Mary remembered that she still hadn't got a pair of tights. If she was going to go to a place where she wanted to make a good first impression, she needed new tights.

Thus, later, when Dad came home from the pub, drunk and went to his room, Meggie and Mary waited, listening for the sound of snoring.

When they were sure he was fast asleep, they tiptoed upstairs, avoiding the treads that they knew from experience had particularly loud creaks. They sneaked up to his bedroom door and opened it, very, very slowly, listening out for him all the while. He did not stir and they crept inside the room, making sure their father was deeply asleep before Mary went to the bedside table.

Upon it were a couple of five-pound notes; she did not dare take these, as they would be likely to be missed; and a large mound of coins from his trouser pockets. As if she were playing spillikins, she removed, with surgical care, a few coins, making great efforts not to disturb the ones that remained in the heap. In all, she managed to collect two pounds. Enough for her tights, a loaf of bread and some breakfast cereal. The stolen money in her hand, she rejoined Meggie and they crept downstairs again to divide the spoils.

'This is great,' was Meggie's opinion. 'We need never go hungry again. It was so *easy*.'

'Yeah,' agreed Mary, with satisfaction. She had enjoyed the escapade. 'It's a good way of getting back at him.'

Meggie and Mary laughed together about it. It proved to be only the first venture into a whole new habit of 'raiding' from their father.

That night, Mary had a dream. In it, she was knocking on doors, asking people if they had seen her mother. At every door the answer was the same: 'No', with a shake of the head and the door closed in her face. Down several deserted streets she went, until, at the far end of one of them, she caught a glimpse of her mother; dark and beautiful, dressed in a tailored suit and high heels.

She called out to her — 'Mum!' but her mother ran away.

Mary chased after her, down the street and several times she saw her out of the corner of her eye, or in the distance, walking away. Tantalisingly, her mother was never any nearer, never any more accessible, no matter how fast Mary ran, or how breathless she became, or how loudly she shouted. Then, unexpectedly, as Mary rounded one more corner she was suddenly within a foot of her mother.

Something was wrong, though. Her mother did not look pleased to see her and her brown eyes were narrowed and hostile.

'Mum — it's me!' pleaded Mary.

Her mother said nothing, pursing her lips as if at a nuisance.

'Mum!' begged Mary. 'It's me!'

Her mother said, 'go away. Go back to your father.'

'No!' yelled Mary desperately.

The dream ended there.

Chapter 19

Comparisons

Gladstone Street Baptist Church was very different from St Patrick's and Mary was stunned. It was like no church she had ever visited. The most obvious differences struck her forcibly as soon as she entered the church with Meggie and Jo and the Fellowes that Sunday.

For a start, there was the building. Where St Pat's had red-brick walls and dark, stained-glass windows, Gladstone Street was a modern, pale blue, painted hall, with large panes of clear glass illuminating the distinctly 'unchurchlike' interior.

Then there was the lack of ecclesiastical ornament. Around the walls of St Pat's were the fourteen stations of the cross; wall plaques depicting Jesus' final journey to Golgotha and the crucifixion. Gladstone Street's walls were bare.

There were no statues here, either. St Pat's had four, with rows of candles in front of each — Our Lady, St Theresa of Avila, the Holy Family (Mary, Joseph and the Baby Jesus) and, of course, St Patrick himself, with snakes around his feet. Gladstone Street did not have so much as a cross above the altar; if a simple wooden table could be described as an altar, whereas St Pat's had a huge one with a plaster figure hanging on it and flanked on either side by smaller statues of Our Lady and Mary Magdalene.

St Patrick's had narrow, dark, wooden pews: Gladstone Street had plastic chairs, with flat cushions.

There were other noticeable dissimilarities; before the service started in Gladstone Street the hall was filled with a murmur and buzz of conversation; in St Pat's, silence reigned before Mass. Mary was also surprised when Susan pointed out the man who was to lead the service and give the sermon. He was wearing a *suit* instead of vestments and was deep in conversation with a member of the congregation. She was more used to the priest, in full regalia, entering the nave in a slow procession with the white-smocked acolytes, accompanied by the fragrance of incense from the swinging censer and a golden crucifix held aloft.

In all, Gladstone Street presented Mary with a considerable culture shock and she was suddenly overcome with an attack of nerves, making her feel claustrophobic and sweaty. All this was so *alien* to her.

She was relieved to sit down in a row on one of the plastic chairs, between Susan and Meggie. Unwittingly, however, she seated herself down upon something hard and had to shift to remove the object. It was a hymnbook. For something to do to relieve her tension, she flicked through it, but recognised very few of the hymns. There were none to

Our Lady, or in honour of any of the Saints and lots
about Jesus.

'Did you bring a Bible?' asked Susan beside her.

Mary looked up.

'No,' she replied bewilderedly, 'I didn't know I
needed one.'

'Oh, it's okay,' Susan reassured her. 'You can look
at mine. Are you all right?'

Mary realised she must appear as stressed as she
felt.

'Yeah, I'm okay,' she answered. 'I just feel a bit
shy.'

Susan smiled crookedly.

'Don't worry,' she told Mary. 'There's no initiation
ceremony for newcomers. No-one's going to ask
you to get up there and give a testimony.'

Mary relaxed slightly and returned the smile,
even though she didn't know what Susan was talking about.

The service began when a small cluster of people,
bearing guitars, appeared near the table and started
to introduce some 'choruses' to the congregation,
who all proceeded to sing heartily, reading the
words from an overhead projector. Again, compari-
sons struck Mary; the congregation at St Pat's were,
she had to admit, feeble singers, whereas these
people seemed to put much more effort into it. She
listened intently to everything that followed, her
curiosity aroused by the 'foreign-ness' of her sur-
roundings and the obvious enthusiasm of the other
celebrants.

After one of the hymns, and prompted by the minister in the suit, Meggie and Jo left the hall to go to Sunday School and Bible Class which was held in an adjoining room. Once the children had left, the main part of the service began.

The Lord's Table, which was the next event, was also a new experience for Mary. Instead of filing out of the rows to be waited on at an altar rail by priest and acolyte, the assembly at Gladstone Street were served in their seats, by suited stewards, with pieces of *real* bread on a silver tray. The celebrants were actually allowed to *finger* this bread, which seemed to Mary to be a sacrilege. At St Pat's the white communion wafer was placed on the tongue of the communicant, or on their palm, to be lifted off with the tongue; the Body of Christ being too sacred a thing to be actually touched with the hand as if it were common *bread*.

Following the bread, wine was served in tiny glass beakers from further silver trays and all the people who had taken the bread, drank the wine. Mary was accustomed to communion wine being drunk from a reverently-held golden chalice by the *priest* and him alone. After all, it was the Blood of Christ.

The sermon, preached with vigour, from a wooden lectern by the man in the suit, impressed Mary with the dramatic and ardent style of its delivery, if not by the content, which went over her head. He preached on a 'minor prophet', unknown to her, the assembly referring to the relevant Bible passages at his direction and there was much emphasis on 'regeneration' and 'justification'; terms new to her.

As the sermon ended and the service eventually drew to a prayerful and meditative close, Mary felt that she had enjoyed it far more than she had expected and felt inexplicably uplifted by the whole experience. When Susan asked her what she had thought of it, she was able to reply with honest delight, 'I liked it! It was different — but I liked it!'

Her friend grinned widely at this ready admission.

That same evening, according to Father Moloney's instruction, Mary attended Mass. It was quiet, subdued, safe and familiar, but, in some ways, it suffered by comparison with Gladstone Street.

Chapter 20

Christian Friends

The next time Mary attended Gladstone Street was a fortnight later, on a Friday. Susan had invited her to the youth club and she decided to accept, partly because she was interested in Susan's friends. She had been introduced to these when she had gone to the Sunday Service and they had appealed to her immediately, not least because the company had included a couple of *boys*.

Now boys were of intense and increasing interest to Mary, a species rare and fascinating and one with which she desired to become better acquainted. There had been boys at primary school, of course, but since then, Mary had had very little contact with that gender. Naturally, boys were excluded from her convent school and she had no brothers, or anything to do with girlfriends' brothers. The only male she currently knew was, in fact, her father. She greatly feared that if she did not begin to socialize with boys very soon she would end her life as an 'old maid' and this anxiety was made even more acute by the fact that Susan had a boyfriend.

Susan's boyfriend was called Andy, a bright-looking boy of fifteen. He was amiable, talkative and clever, with brown eyes and dark blond hair. He dressed in dirty denim, with old trainers on his feet and a black T-shirt under his jacket.

Dave was slightly younger than Andy, slightly taller and as retiring as Andy was extroverted. He had soft, light brown hair and grey eyes and dressed more tidily and cleanly than did his friend.

The other member of Susan's gang was Alison, a tall, well-built fourteen-year-old, very trendy, outspoken and confident, with a pale skin and very dark hair and eyes. She liked to wear make-up and short skirts.

The thing that attracted Mary to the group as a whole was their air of happiness and that indefinable aura of 'light' she had first noticed when she met Susan — that inner radiance that drew her, as a moth to a candle.

The Friday Club was held each week in a room on the other side of the church's entrance foyer from the main hall. It was simply furnished, with wooden tables and plastic chairs, like the ones in the church and it was about the size of the average classroom. The walls were painted a gentle, sun-yellow and there was a dark blue, wall-to-wall carpet. A large window looked onto a view of the church car park and a few small trees brushed their leaves against the glass.

The Friday Club meeting took the form of a Bible study, followed by group discussion.

Andy was holding a sheet of paper as Mary, with Susan and her friends, sat around a table. He read out to the group one of the typed questions on it while, around them, similar groups did the same.

There was a sound of animated conversation.

'It says here,' began Andy, his pen poised above the page ready to write down their answers, 'do you think, after hearing the study on Proverbs chapter twenty, verse one and Proverbs chapter twenty-three, verse twenty and twenty-nine to thirty-five, that Christians should drink alcohol?'

'No,' stated Alison decisively, 'it's obvious.'

'I don't agree,' put in Andy.

'How can you not agree!' remonstrated Alison, good-naturedly. 'It says: "Do not join with those who drink too much wine"!'

'Yeah, *too much*,' rejoined her friend. 'Not *none*. Just *too much*.'

'Yeah,' said Dave more gently. 'It doesn't say you're not to drink at all. It just says you're not to drink *too much*. That doesn't mean you have to go teetotal.'

Susan spoke up in Alison's defence.

'But if drink's such a dangerous thing, maybe it's best to avoid it altogether.'

'It's only dangerous to alcoholics,' said Andy. Susan and Mary looked uncomfortable at this.

'Okay,' reasoned Alison, 'but if you don't find out who's an alcoholic and who isn't until one of them's hooked on the stuff, then isn't it better to avoid it, just in case?'

David said, 'isn't that a bit like saying you're not going to walk down the street in case you get mugged?'

'No,' Alison replied unruffled, 'it's not the same thing at all. Some risks you have to take, others you don't.'

'Mmm ...'

A musing silence fell.

'Okay,' said Andy, breaking it. 'I'll put down "opinion divided" for that one.' He wrote down their answer on the typed sheet and read out the next question. 'Is alcoholism a disease?'

'A disease?' repeated Susan after a moment's thought. 'Of course it is.'

'It doesn't say that in the Bible,' objected Dave mildly.

'But it's a commonly accepted fact, isn't it? It's a medical fact.'

'It doesn't call it a disease in the Bible.'

'No ...,' said Susan, 'but maybe they just didn't understand about things like that in those days.'

Alison drew in her breath sharply.

'Watch it,' she told Susan.

'Pardon?'

'If the Bible says it's a *sin* to drink too much, then it's a *sin* and it can't be an *illness*, 'cos it's not a sin to be ill.'

'You've got me there,' admitted Susan with a rueful smile.

Dave looked at Mary.

'What do you think?' he asked her. 'You look like you've got some thoughts on the subject.'

'Do I?'

Mary winced nervously, realising her face had given her thoughts away once again.

'Well,' she began awkwardly, 'I have really. I've thought about it myself, when people like psychologists and that say it's a disease and the alcoholics can't help it. I'm not so sure. People *choose* to drink, don't they? It's their *choice*. You can't *choose* to be ill. It'd be a funny sort of disease where you *chose* to be ill. Calling it a disease is like an excuse. That's what I think, anyway,' she concluded apologetically.

'What shall I put then?' queried Andy, waggling his biro.

'Put, "we don't know",' advised Dave. 'We'll have to pass on that one.'

'Can I ask something?' Mary questioned as Andy wrote.

'Yeah,' answered Susan.

'Why do you bother with the Bible so much? If you want to find out about alcoholism, wouldn't you be better off reading a book that's actually *about* alcoholism?'

The friends glanced at each other wryly. Susan explained for them.

'We believe, as Christians, that the Bible is the Word of God, that what it says is true and that it can tell us all we need to know about anything, if we know where to look for the answer. That's why we study it.'

'But not *all* Christians believe the Bible. *I* don't.'

The group seemed to tense slightly at this statement. Then Susan spoke again, somewhat cautiously.

'Don't you believe any of it?'

'Some bits,' conceded Mary, 'but it's not the "be all and end all". The Pope has the last word in my church.'

There was another pause, then Dave asked her, 'have you always been a Christian, Mary?'

'Of course!' she replied with surprise. 'I was christened as a baby!'

At this point, the youth leader called the roomful of people to silence and the discussion was ended as he began to speak to them all again. The topic of 'Bible-believing' prematurely closed, Mary felt oddly out of tune, now, with Susan's gang. She felt that she and they were not on quite the same wavelength.

She was right.

Chapter 21

Birthday Plans

Mary had written to seven addresses from her mother's diary and of these, six had replied. None had had phone numbers, though Mary would have been unable to ring anyway, with the local phoneboxes vandalised and their own phone cut off.

The first three letters had been posted to members of the Dawe (her mother's) family in Lancashire. The returning post informed Mary, politely enough, that she ought to mind her own business and that they were very sorry to have to say so. Mary had expected this response, which was why she had not limited her correspondence to relatives, but had extended it to include personal friends of her mother.

The fourth reply was from an old schoolfriend in Kent, who told Mary that she had not seen her mother for several years and that they had no contact anyway beyond the exchange of birthday and Christmas cards.

The fifth turned out to be more a friend of Brian's than of her mother and he, too, said that his relationship with 'the couple' had lapsed.

The sixth was a lecturer from a teacher training

college, who said he had no idea where Mary's mother was and had never even heard of Brian.

The seventh letter fell on even stonier ground. There was no reply to it after an interval of six weeks.

During this period of time, however, Mary had been distracted by the development of her own social contacts at Gladstone Street, so she had not found the wait for replies too difficult.

Through Gladstone Street, she had become friendly with Alison, Andy and Dave, as well as getting to know Susan better and all this had helped her to feel less lonely.

She had formed the habit of going to Gladstone Street Youth Club on a Friday night, Gladstone Street again on a Sunday morning and Mass on a Sunday evening. This, she knew in the back of her mind, was a compromise that would not last.

She felt guilty about the fact that she was so keen to attend Gladstone Street and so *dutiful* to attend St Patrick's. She felt too guilty about her growing preference, in fact, to admit as much to Father Moloney, much as she liked him.

Gladstone Street seemed to Mary to be so much more welcoming than St Pat's, where her only friend was a man of the cloth. At Gladstone Street she could talk to people her own age and she could actually enjoy herself. She told herself, by way of an excuse, that she needed all the enjoyment she could get, just to keep herself sane and help her to cope with the dreadfulness of her home environment. And yet, she still wanted to remain a Catholic, out of loyalty, as well as a love, for the 'institution' that had educated and formed her from infancy. After all, it wasn't so much a case of turning anti-Catholic as pro-Gladstone Street.

It was such a shame Gladstone Street was Protestant. She had always believed that Protestants were inevitably going to hell, simply because they committed the sin of not being Catholic. Yet it seemed a very harsh judgment to make on people who were *easily* as devout as her own kind.

These thoughts were turning over in her mind as she made herself a cup of tea in the Hanrahans' kitchen, her teaspoon squeezing all the remaining strength out of a tea-bag on its second cuppa.

'Has he bought any *more* tea-bags yet?' queried Meggie as she entered the grubby room.

'No.'

'Have you told him we're out of them?' she continued as she rooted in the larder cupboard for coffee.

'Twice.'

Meggie tutted impatiently.

'We'll have to nick some more money off him again tonight, then,' she complained as she made herself a drink.

'Yeah. Okay.'

'Still no reply to that last letter?'

'No.'

Mary blinked as she tried to concentrate on what Meggie was saying.

'I think I'll go round there,' she said.

'Will you?' rejoined Meggie, with interest.

'Yeah. You can come if you like. It's only a bus ride away. I want to "eliminate it from my enquiries" as the police say. It's a fairly recent entry in her diary, so there might be some clues there.'

'It's worth checking,' agreed her sister. 'I'll come with you. Oh, and Clare rang from school.'

'Oh yeah? What did she want?'

'She said Jill and she are going to the disco on Saturday night and do you want to come.'

Mary groaned.

'I've been meaning to "creep" to Dad about that,' she told Meggie. 'Jill and Clare started going there a few weeks ago, but I haven't dared ask *him* if I can go. I just *know* he'll say no.'

'He's bound to.'

'Still,' mused Mary aloud, 'it's my birthday next week.'

'Fourteen!' said Meggie, with mock horror. 'You're getting really *old*, Mary.'

'Cheers,' her sister responded bitterly. 'I might as well take advantage of it, though.'

'What do you mean?'

'I mean he might feel he's got to be extra nice to me if it's my birthday, so I might be able to wheedle permission out of him to go to the disco.'

Meggie looked doubtful.

'Worth trying, I suppose,' she said nevertheless. 'Has he asked you what you want for your birthday?'

'No,' answered Mary in a puzzled tone of voice.

'No, he hasn't this year. What are *you* getting me?'

Meggie snorted scornfully in response and left the kitchen.

As Mary drank her tea, she carried on wondering what to do about the disco. Jill and Clare had said the 'Angel Arms' was great and they had *both* found boyfriends there, which made Mary think Jill and Clare were probably right.

The only obstacle to her going there was Dad.

Chapter 22

Happy Birthday?

Mary's fourteenth birthday, which fell on June 10th, was unlike any other birthday she had ever known. In the old days, when the family was still united and comfortably off, birthdays had been grand celebrations, including certain rituals which, although she had taken them pretty much for granted at the time, she now ached for.

The first thing she missed was the joyous rush of the rest of the family into her bedroom, singing 'Happy Birthday To You' at the tops of their voices and showering her with gaily-wrapped presents. This year, she got up in the morning as if it were any other weekend morning and went downstairs on her own, wondering if her family could really have *forgotten* it was her birthday. There was no-one in the kitchen cooking her special birthday fried breakfast and no little stack of birthday mail for her on the dining table. She got her own bowl of cereal ready and took it to the table herself. Some sense of expectation had caused her, on her birthday morning, to rise early, but there was nothing in the silent house to indicate that her family were even awake yet.

Feeling extremely sorry for herself, she sat down

at the greasy table, stirring the cereal and milk in her bowl, until she heard bumping about from upstairs and the sound of her sisters' footsteps descending.

'Happy Birthday!' cried Meggie and Jo, happily, as they entered the dining room, bearing a small parcel each.

'Oh!'

Mary was glad and relieved that they had not forgotten.

'We got you presents!' Jo told her gleefully.

'Oh — thanks,' said Mary, gratefully, as she took them.

She opened the little packets. Jo had given her a packet of mints and Meggie had given her a pencil case.

'That's great — thanks ever such a lot!' she cried. 'They're lovely!'

'Sorry it isn't much,' apologised Meggie.

'No — it's fine, really! Thanks!'

Mary knew that Meggie knew that the gifts were a come-down when compared with those of earlier years. In earlier years, Mum would have given each of the younger girls a few pounds to buy Mary presents and — but never mind. Mary really *did* appreciate the presents her sisters had bought her out of the little they had and there was simply no point in remembering how things *used* to be. Besides, it wasn't the lavish gifts she really missed, but one of the givers — her mother.

Mum had not even sent a card.

Even though Mary reasoned that her mother

couldn't send a card if she didn't know where they lived, for some reason she had been holding out the hope that the postman would bring *something* from Mum. At that moment, Mary would have sacrificed all the birthday presents she ever had for the sake of that one card.

While Meggie and Jo were having their breakfast at the table with Mary, their father came downstairs. He looked sheepish and held an unwrapped box in his hands. Mary could tell from the pictures on the box that it was a camera.

'I didn't have time to wrap it,' he announced, sounding sorry as he put the box down on the table. 'It's a camera. I thought you might like one. You're old enough. Happy Birthday.'

Mary found this little speech rather touching. Her father was trying to be nice.

'Oh — thanks Dad,' she smiled as she drew the box towards her across the table. 'It's great — just what I wanted. Thanks ever such a lot. Has it got a film in?'

'Yes,' answered her father. 'There's one in the box. You look after that, mind. It's an expensive one. The camera, I mean.'

'Oh yes, I'm sure,' agreed Mary eagerly.

For a second, their eyes met and it was as if Mary and her father were reaching out to each other, but were afraid to touch. Mr Hanrahan was the first to look away.

'Dying for a cup of tea,' he muttered as he made his way through to the kitchen.

The three girls opened the box and poured over

the new camera, fiddling with it, turning it over in their hands and attempting to make sense of the instructions.

'It's really nice,' whispered Meggie, as if she had made a secret confession that their father must not hear.

'I know,' nodded Mary conspiratorially.

After a time, Meggie and Jo went through to the front room to watch TV, leaving Mary in the dining room and Dad next door in the kitchen, the connecting door ajar.

Mary knew that this was her best opportunity to ask about the disco, even though she also knew that to raise the subject involved the risk of breaking the spell of birthday harmony. She got up from the table and went into the kitchen, where her father was making himself some toast.

'I really like the camera, Dad,' she began.

'Good,' he said, sounding pleased.

'Dad . . .,' she continued fearfully. 'Jill and Clare have asked me to a — to a disco for Saturday night and I'd really like to go. Can I?'

Mr Hanrahan looked up sharply, suddenly alert. 'What?' he rejoined disbelievingly. 'A *disco*?'

'Yes.'

'Not on your nelly,' was his curt answer, as he crossly buttered his toast. 'Those are dreadful places. I wouldn't have expected any daughter of mine to want to be seen *dead* in one of those places.'

'But I want to go,' she pleaded.

'Ha! These places are where tarts and sluts hang

out, waiting to be picked up,' he informed her
derisively. 'No member of *this* family ought to be
seen there. It's a pick-up joint, that's all it is. A
pick-up joint.'

'Please Dad,' Mary begged. 'Jill and Clare are
going ...'

'*No*! I forbid it absolutely.' He checked himself, as
a thought occurred to him. 'I suppose you thought
I'd let you, did you, because it's your birthday?'

Mary swallowed guiltily.

'Ha!' exclaimed her father. 'How dare you take
advantage of my good nature like that! You must
think I was born yesterday!' He continued to butter
his toast with angry vigour. 'Well you can't go and
that's flat! Do you want to make a slut of yourself —
do you?'

'N — no,' replied his daughter nervously. 'But —.'

'But *nothing*! You're never to set so much as a
foot in one of these places and if I ever hear — ' he
waved his butter-knife at her in fury ' — if I ever
hear that you *have* been — then you're out of this
house! Out on your ear! Your precious Fellowes can
look after you, because I just won't want to know!
My goodness, I should have deposited you on the
Social Services while I had the chance.'

With that, he stormed out of the kitchen, carrying
his breakfast with him on a plate. So agitated was
he that he jolted a piece of toast off the plate and it
fell, butter-side-down, onto the dirty carpet of the
dining room. He shouted back at Mary lividly, 'Now
look what you made me do!'

Mary might have levelled the same accusation

back at him, for she made up her mind, there and then, that she *would* go to the disco, with or without his permission.

Chapter 23

Mary's Boyfriend

'It wasn't like I expected.'

Mary was describing her first experience of the local disco to Susan, as they sat together on the tidy bed in Mary's small bedroom. Mary's bedroom was not like the other rooms in that house. Away from the destructive influence of the rest of her family, she was able to keep it clean and neat. On the polished, wooden surfaces of the chest and dressing table were tiny crocheted mats which had been made by her mother. Small pottery ornaments were arranged on these white mats and there was a glass vase of garden flowers on the bedside table, next to the lamp and alarm clock.

She had sneaked out to the 'Angel Arms' that Saturday night after her father had departed for the pub and she had returned home before he did, so that he did not suspect her disobedience. Meggie had been willingly sworn to secrecy about the escapade and Susan had also, reluctantly, promised not to tell.

'What *did* you expect, then?' rejoined the plumper girl, with a slightly bemused expression.

'I thought it'd be fun, like Jill and Clare said it would. They said it was great; a really good laugh, but I didn't like it at all.'

'Why?'

Mary sighed, with frustration, as she tried to explain her feelings.

'I just — didn't like it,' she told her friend. 'I just felt — terrible — there.'

'I reckon I would too,' agreed Susan.

'Have you ever been, then?'

Susan gave a short laugh.

'You're kidding. Mum wouldn't let me and anyway I wouldn't really want to go.'

'But *everyone* goes to discos!' objected Mary.

Susan shook her head.

'They don't,' she said. 'I know lots of people who don't. Dave and Andy and Alison don't.'

'Don't they?' asked Mary with surprise.

'No. Their parents — well, and Andy's stepmum — he's adopted — they wouldn't let them.'

Mary was bewildered.

'And don't they *mind*?' she queried.

'Who, Dave and Andy and Alison?'

'Yeah.'

'No. They feel the way I do. Besides, we've got other things. Things that we enjoy just as much. We have Barn Dances sometimes at our church. You'll have to come to the next one.'

Mary nodded and Susan continued with interest, 'but tell me what happened at the disco.'

Mary lay back on her bed and put her hands behind her head as she gazed up at the cracked, once-white ceiling. Susan leaned on one elbow as she prepared to listen to the story.

'Well,' began Mary, 'we got there, right, and paid to go in.'

'What did you wear?' interrupted Susan.

Mary shrugged.

'My best stuff. I didn't look as good as Jill and Clare though.'

'Go on.'

'Well,' continued Mary, 'we went in and there were loads of people there and flashing lights and the music was really loud — good, but loud. There was a bar and tables all around. We had to say we were sixteen to get in, but there were lots of other people there our age.'

'Did you get in easily?'

'Yeah, very easy. Anyway, we bought a drink — it was really dear — and we stood about for a bit, looking round.'

'Weren't Jill and Clare's boyfriends there?'

'No, they weren't,' answered Mary.

'Go on.'

'Anyway, when we'd finished our drinks we went and danced.'

'Just you three girls?'

'Yeah. I hated that bit.'

'Why?'

'I can't dance. I didn't know what to do with my hands. I felt really stupid, just trying to dance. I felt like an idiot. I think I'll smoke next time, like Jill and Clare do. It gives you something to do with your hands and it looks good.'

'No!' gasped Susan, shocked. 'Don't do that!'

Mary merely shrugged again in response, feeling stupid once more.

'Anyway, in the end these three boys came up and asked us to dance. They looked older than us — about eighteen.'

'Really!'

Mary smiled roguishly, thinking she had impressed Susan at last.

'Mine was really nice-looking,' she went on. 'Tall and blond. He's called Kev. Anyway, he asked me out.'

'*Did* he?'

'Yeah,' Mary said proudly. 'I'm meeting him in the market square tomorrow night.'

There was a pause, as Susan digested this information. Then she said seriously:

'You mustn't go, Mary.'

Mary laughed, not understanding.

'Why ever not?'

Susan spread her hands imploringly.

'Because you don't *know* him,' she insisted. 'You don't know anything about him, or what he's done, or — or where he's *been*.'

The friends looked at each other, communicating, without words. Mary knew what Susan was trying to tell her.

'But I like Kev,' she said lamely.

'You don't know him,' retorted Susan.

'Not *yet*.'

'How well do you *want* to know him?'

'What do you mean by that?'

Susan tutted.

'What I mean is — look, he's eighteen. Are you ready for —.' She lowered her voice. 'For *that* yet?'

Mary felt embarrassed now and very silly indeed.

'I — I don't know,' she replied. In fact, although she would not admit it even to herself, she knew she was not ready for *that*.

Susan sat up and adopted a gentler, more reasoning tone.

'Look,' she explained. 'It's much safer if you go out with people you actually know, like Andy and I, although we don't actually *go out* as such 'cos we're too young. I've known Andy all my life. It'd be much better for you, for instance, if you went out with Dave, or someone like that, whose background you know something about. Kev's a totally unknown quantity, isn't he?'

Mary sat up too and hung her head.

'But I'd really like to have a boyfriend,' she said miserably.

Susan gave a sympathetic sigh.

'Look,' she said, 'I understand all that, but — there's a right way and a wrong way and you're going about it the wrong way.'

Mary pursed her lips, beginning to feel that she was being preached at.

'It's all very well for you to talk,' she told Susan. 'You know lots of boys and you've *got* a boyfriend anyway. Besides, don't *you* kiss him and that? How can you tell me I'm not ready for all that when *you* do it?'

'I don't,' admitted Susan matter-of-factly.

'No?' repeated Mary, with incredibility.

'*No.*'

'I don't believe you.'

'Well, it's true. It's the church. There are some things that people don't do, 'cos of our beliefs and that's one of them, for us fourteen-year-olds anyway.'

Mary was astonished.

'Honest?' she breathed.

'Honest.'

'Wow.'

As Mary considered this restrained conduct, she discovered, to her own surprise, that she found the 'Gladstone Street' boy-girl behaviour quite appealing. In Susan's world, there would be no dangers, fewer risks, no pressure to do things you didn't want to do, nothing to fear. Susan's world was clean and safe and not like the dark, secretive, too-adult world of the 'Angel Arms'.

'Please don't go out with Kev,' urged Susan. 'Just stand him up. He can take it.'

Mary combed her fingers through her mousey hair, closing her eyes as she admitted defeat.

'Okay,' she said quietly.

Chapter 24

Who Is Mrs Patel?

Mary was beginning to see Susan in a new light; as a protectress. Her intervention in the 'affair' of Kev had, Mary now felt, preserved her from a fate worse than death and she was duly grateful. Looking back, she marvelled that, in the first place, she could have been so easily ensnared by the immoral lifestyle surrounding the 'Angel Arms'. After all, even while she had been there, she had loathed it and now that Susan had offered her a more wholesome and healthy method of achieving the same end, i.e. to get a boyfriend, she had one more reason to go to Gladstone Street.

For the time being, however, she was chiefly concerned with the search for her mother and to that end, one Sunday afternoon, Meggie and she found themselves on a number seventy-five bus, heading in the direction of the seventh address.

'I wonder who this Mrs Patel is?' Meggie said.

They were sitting in a twin seat on the half-empty top deck, as the red bus chugged away from Backmount Road and into a more pleasant suburb. Mary retrieved the relevant diary from her cardigan pocket and flicked through it 'til she found the appropriate entry.

'"Mrs Patel"' she quoted. '"12a Lansdowne Terrace, Bromley." Mrs Patel must be the lady who lives there.'

'She must be Indian or something. Do you think she speaks English?'

Mary raised her eyes heavenward and gave a crooked grin.

'Don't be daft,' she told her sister. 'If she didn't speak English, she couldn't be a friend of Mum's, could she? Unless Mum speaks Indian, which she doesn't.'

'Oh yeah,' said Meggie. ''Course.'

'What was your Bible Class like this morning?'

Meggie pulled a face.

'Bit boring,' she replied frankly. 'It was about the Old Testament. I nearly fell asleep. I think I'll stop going.'

Mary was surprised.

'Will you? But I thought you liked it.'

'I *did*,' corrected her sister, 'but the novelty's worn off a bit and I'm fed up with getting stick from Dad about it.'

Mary nodded, with understanding.

'What about Jo?' she asked. 'Does she like Sunday School?'

Meggie shrugged.

'For the time being, yeah. But if I stop going she might stop, too. What about you?'

'Well, I'm going,' Mary declared. 'I'm really getting into it. Alison's asked me to the pictures with her and Dave next week. Dad won't let me go, of course, 'cos they're Protestants and he doesn't know them, but I'll just do what I did when I went to the "Angel Arms".'

'Yeah. That worked quite well.'

There was a pause, as the bus idled at traffic lights.

'Mind you,' continued Mary, 'I still wish Dad'd give it a rest. The way he goes on about Gladstone Street, anyone'd think it was a witches' coven.'

Meggie gave a grunt of agreement.

'I think we want the next stop,' said Mary. 'Come on, let's go down.'

They made their way down the narrow staircase of the moving bus and rang the bell to signal the driver to stop, then dismounted into a wide avenue of 'between-wars' semis.

It was a sunny, warm day and the roses in the front gardens of the well-maintained mock-Tudor houses were pink and pretty. There was a buzz of insects and a washing of cars in the driveways of some of the houses.

'This is like where we used to live,' commented Mary wistfully.

'Yeah,' sighed Meggie. 'What number did we want?'

'12a. We're on the right side of the road.'

They strolled down the pavement, under the shade of sycamores, enjoying the change of scene, until they arrived at the black-painted iron gate of number 12a.

It was a house like any of the others, clean and comfortable-looking and there was a red Mini parked in front of the wooden garage to the side of the house. At the smart doorway there were three separate bells, indicating that the property had been divided into flats. The two lower doorbells were labelled with names that meant nothing to the girls and the top one was blank.

'The top one must be Mrs Patel's,' suggested Mary.

'Try it.'

Mary pressed the bell and they could hear the sound of it ringing at the top of the house.

There was no answer. Mary tried it again and again, but there was still no answer. Irritated, she said, 'that was a wasted journey,' then she had an idea and pressed one of the other bells.

Unfortunately, that too seemed to fall on deaf ears, as did the last one.

'They're all out,' stated Meggie.

'I gathered that,' retorted her sister. 'Come on, let's go home.'

Disappointed, the two girls went to the nearest bus stop and caught a bus returning to Backmount Road.

Mary called in at the Fellowes' rather than go straight home and Jean opened the door to her.

'Hello love,' smiled Susan's mother. 'How are you? Do you want Susan?'

'Yes, please.'

'She's in her own room. Go on up.'

'Thanks.'

Mary mounted the carpeted stairs to her friend's bedroom and knocked at the door.

'Come in!' called a cheerful voice and Mary entered the room.

It was similar, in some ways, to her own bedroom. Susan took a pride in her private space and was also fond of small ornaments, only Susan had decked surfaces of white chipboard, rather than Mary's polished wood. Susan's bedroom walls were covered in pop posters and, oddly, to Mary, illustrated Bible texts.

She sat down on the quilted bed with Susan, as she had many times before and told her friend about her fruitless return bus journey.

'So this Mrs Patel lives in the top flat, does she?' said Susan when Mary had finished her tale.

'She must do. Her name is with the address.'

'They must be rented flats,' observed Susan, for no particular reason.

'Yes.'

Mary realised something suddenly and gave a start.

'Rented!' she exclaimed, her grey eyes widening.

'So?' rejoined Susan, with a querying tilt of the head.

'Well, if they're rented, then there must be a landlord — or land*lady*!'

'I suppose so,' agreed Susan, still missing the point.

'Well — don't you see? If Mrs Patel's name wasn't on the doorbell, then maybe she doesn't live there at all! Maybe she's just the landlady!'

'The landlady?' repeated Susan, trying to follow Mary's train of thought.

'*Yes!*' enthused Mary. 'If Mrs Patel is the landlady and Mum had her name and address, then maybe Mum is the *tenant*! Maybe *Mum* lives on the top flat!'

Chapter 25

Mary Has An Idea

After Mary withdrew from the 'Angel Arms' scene, she noticed Jill and Clare withdrawing from her. Her decision to opt out of that way of night-time socialising seemed to mark a departure point in her school friendships and an increasing dependence upon her Gladstone Street friends, especially Susan. She wasn't entirely sorry to lose Jill and Clare. Ever since her parents separated, she had felt that there was a breach between them. It was easier to feel comfortable with people who knew her the way she lived now rather than the way she used to be. In the same way, it was easier to be frank and open with her new friends and confide in them as she had not confided with Jill and Clare.

Thus, she found herself, one evening, in the crowded church room before the start of Friday Club, telling them about her quest for her mother and the latest development regarding 12a Lansdowne Terrace.

The reactions of her friends were mixed. All of them agreed that there was a strong chance her theory about Mrs Patel was right, but they differed when it came to the eventual outcome of the search, presuming Mary really did manage to trace her mother.

131

'You ought to brace yourself,' advised Dave thoughtfully as he twiddled a pencil.

They were all sitting on one of the tables.

'Why?' asked Mary.

'Well,' explained the softly-spoken boy. 'It strikes me your mother's at great pains to hide herself.'

'Yeah,' objected Alison, 'but she's probably only hiding from Mary's dad. We've all heard what *he's* like. Anyway, it might not be that she's *hiding*. She might be looking for Mary and her sisters right now and she can't find them 'cos they've moved.'

'Surely she could find them,' said Andy with a frown. 'If she wanted to find them, she'd just have to ask the school, or the D.S.S. They've got Child Benefit books, so their present address would be on their records at the D.S.S.'

'But maybe she just never thought to ask the D.S.S.,' countered Alison.

'It's unlikely.'

There was a pause, then Mary spoke.

'Look,' she began, 'I know there's all sorts of questions and things that don't tie up, but — it comes back to this: Would any mother willingly abandon her children on a man she knew to be a heavy drinker and whom she didn't trust? The answer has to be no, so there must be a *reason* why I can't get to her right now.'

'If there's a good reason,' put in Susan, 'then maybe you'd be better off just leaving it.'

'I can't!' exclaimed Mary. 'She's my mother! I've got to find her, so that I can talk to her and find out what's been going on.'

At this point the youth leaders entered the

room and the volume of conversation amongst the various groups dropped as the older ones began to unroll a large piece of paper.

'When are you going to go back to the house in Bromley?' asked Alison in a low voice, as the youth leaders attached the paper to the wall with sticky tack.

'Tomorrow. Meggie and I are going.'

'If you do find your Mum,' said Susan, with caution, 'you'll have a job keeping it from your Dad. If he finds out he'll be really angry.'

Mary shrugged, pretending not to care.

'I'll cross that bridge when I come to it.'

Susan looked worried and spoke to her friend in a confidential whisper.

'Listen,' she began, 'I've promised I won't tell, or anything, but I don't like keeping this sort of secret. It puts me in a bit of an awkward position. I mean, you're going against your Dad's orders and — I know he's really difficult and everything — but if my Mum found out what I'm doing she'd be furious.'

'I know,' said Mary. 'I'm sorry, but there's no reason why she should find out and I really need someone I can trust. You won't tell, will you?'

'No. No, I won't. But I still feel bad about this.'

'Don't worry,' Mary said persuasively. 'If your Mum ever *did* find out I'll say I *made* you keep the secret and then you'll be "let off the hook". I really need someone I can rely on right now and you're the only friend I can trust.'

The youth leaders called the room to order and the conversation ended as the study began.

There were two leaders for that evening's session

and, as usual, they divided the supervision of the activities between them. This week, Alice was obviously down to do the games, for she remained seated while Pete did the study.

Pete was about twenty-five, a short, dark-haired man of slight build. He had an RAF-style moustache and sticking-out ears. Mary liked his ears. When Pete stood with his back to the window, as he now was, the sunlight shone through his ears, so that they appeared to glow.

'Turn in your Bibles to Acts two, verse thirty-eight,' he instructed brightly. 'I thought tonight we'd talk about believers' baptism, as some of you have been asking about it.'

Mary was pleased Pete had chosen this subject. She had heard of it and was curious to know what the term meant. Pete read out the text.

' "Repent and be baptised, every one of you",' he quoted. 'Well, that's clear enough. But can anyone explain fully what is required before baptism?'

There was a brief silence, as the occupants of the room glanced at each other to see who would supply the answer.

After a moment, Andy put up his hand.

'You have to believe in the Lord Jesus Christ for the forgiveness of your sins.'

'Correct,' agreed Pete. 'Now, who can tell me *how* the Lord Jesus Christ forgives our sins?'

'Through the sacrifice of the cross,' replied someone else.

'Yes.'

Pete pointed up at the paper on the wall.

'This is an illustration of how it works.'

The wall chart had a simple drawing, in felt pen, on it. There were two cliff edges opposite to each other, one labelled 'God' and the other 'Man'. The word 'Sin' occupied the gap between the cliffs and a cross-shape formed a bridge between them.

'Just as you can only get from one cliff to the other by means of the bridge,' explained Pete, 'the only way man — you — can get near to God is via Christ. "Your sins have separated you from God", Isaiah, the prophet, tells us. Sin is the gap between the cliffs and the only way to bridge the gap is by believing that Christ's blood cleanses you from the stain of all your sins. Nothing you can *do* can bring you close to God. The only thing that can bring you into friendship with God is your faith in the power of Christ's blood. "It is by grace you have been saved, through faith", we read in Ephesians two, "and this not from yourselves, it is the gift of God". It doesn't matter how good you try to be to make up for your sins. "Your good deeds are like filthy rags", it says in Isaiah — and it doesn't matter how guilty you feel, or even how much you ask for forgiveness from God. Unless you really believe that Christ is the bridge — "for there is no other name under heaven given to men by which we must be saved", the book of Acts states — the stain of your sins cannot be removed. Any questions?'

There appeared to be none, then someone said, 'but we've heard all this before, Pete.'

Pete suppressed a smile.

'I can never take it for granted that you believe it,

though,' he said. 'There's just another text I'll throw at you. "There is one mediator between God and men, the man Christ Jesus". You'll find it in 1 Timothy 2, but what does it mean?'

Susan answered, 'it means that if you pray to anyone other than God himself, through Christ, then your prayers will not be heard.'

'Who can't you pray to, then?'

'Well,' shrugged Susan, 'anyone else, I suppose, except Christ. I suppose you can't pray to believers who have died.'

'Exactly. Thank you.'

Mary's attention had wandered off during this discourse, but she began to listen again as the talk returned to the subject of believers' baptism.

Pete said, 'you can't become a member of this *particular* church family unless you've been baptised as a believer — and I don't mean as a baby. Some other Christian churches do have different views on this, however, but here, you must satisfy our elders that you are truly "in the faith" before you can be baptised.'

'Thought Police,' came a mutter from a corner of the room.

Pete sighed patiently.

'If we didn't *check*,' he insisted, 'we might end up with a membership full of non-believers.'

The heckler grunted.

'Where was I?' queried Pete. 'Oh yes. So who would like to define believers' baptism for me?'

Alison put her hand up.

'It's when you decide that Christ died for you

personally and has forgiven your sins and it's a sign to the church — and to everyone else — that you've come to faith.'

'Perfect.'

Pete went on to talk about something else, but Mary was lost in thought. 'A member of Gladstone Street?' she pondered. If she were to do that, it would mean excommunication from the Catholic Church, which meant hell, if that were true. Yet — it was obvious that the only way to be really 'in' with Gladstone Street was to become a member, like her new friends were. She did not want to sit on the fence forever. Unless she became a member of Gladstone Street, she would always be a visitor; a guest, never fully a part of it. But before you could become a member, you had to be baptised as a believer. Well, Mary knew she was a believer — she always had been — so why not get baptised as one?

Chapter 26

Disaster

It was a rainy, Saturday when Mary and Meggie returned to 12a Lansdowne Terrace and heavy drops of water were falling from the dark leaves of the sycamores, onto the wet pavement.

As before, the girls went through the black iron gate and passed the red Mini as they walked to the door. Their umbrellas dripping, they sheltered under the porch and regarded the line of doorbells.

'Go on, then,' urged Meggie.

'Okay.'

Mary pressed the button that had no label and they waited. There was no sound from within the house, so she pressed again. After some moments, it was obvious that no-one was going to answer.

'Now what?' asked Meggie.

'We try another one.'

Mary pressed one of the two remaining bells and, presently, heard a sound of footsteps on stairs. A pale shape became visible behind the glass of the door which now opened.

'Yes?'

The speaker was a girl in her twenties, dressed like a student and with dyed blonde hair.

'Can I help you?' she enquired curiously.

Mary and Meggie looked at each other, then Mary spoke.

'We're looking for someone,' she began timidly. 'Is there a lady here called Mrs Hanrahan?'

'Mrs Hanrahan?' repeated the girl. 'No. There's only me here at the moment and Steve in the other flat. The couple who have just moved into the top flat are out.'

Mary's ears pricked up.

'What's their name?' she asked. 'It isn't Patel, is it?'

'No,' frowned the girl. 'Look — what do you want?'

'Please — what's the name of the couple on the top flat?'

The girl shrugged her shoulders.

'Oh well,' she sighed, 'I suppose there's no real reason why I shouldn't tell you. Their name is Powell.'

Mary's heart sank. She knew no-one of that name.

'Look — who are you?' asked the girl suspiciously. 'Are you friends of theirs?'

Mary nodded dismally, then said, 'could you tell me what *Mrs* Powell looks like?'

The girl considered the question.

'Well . . .,' she began carefully. 'I've only seen her once or twice, but . . . let me see. She's average height, with dark brown, long hair. Dark eyes, I think and tanned skin. Dresses very smartly, as if she works in an office. High heels, good make-up. She's a very attractive woman, really, for her age.'

Mary could barely restrain her excitement and

she gasped out loud. The girl had just given an accurate description of her mother!

'Is anything wrong?' asked the girl, scrutinising the young callers, who both bore the same astonished expression.

'N — n — no,' answered Mary breathlessly. 'No. . . . Please, when will she be home?'

The girl shook her head.

'No idea,' she replied. 'She and her husband are out quite a lot.'

Meggie spoke up.

'What's her husband's name?' she enquired.

'Oh — he's called Brian. Her name is Jessica.'

That was it, then. There was no doubt but that their mother and Brian were living as man and wife in the top flat and that Mary and Meggie had finally managed to find their whereabouts.

'Do you want to leave a message?' asked the girl.

Mary looked again at Meggie.

'Should we?' asked the younger sister.

Mary paused as she thought about it.

'No,' she decided at last, turning back to the student. 'No, it's OK, we'll call back. Oh — do you have a phone number?'

'Yes. Here — I'll write it down for you.'

The girl disappeared back into the house and re-emerged holding a scrap of paper with the phone number written on it.

'It's best to try in the evenings,' she advised.

'Okay. Thank you,' said Mary and the girls hurriedly left the mystified student, who wondered about them long after they had gone.

Back at home, the sisters were still in a state of

high excitement and had difficulty calming their
mood for the sake of their father and younger sister.
Jo, of course, could not be trusted with the secret.

Unfortunately, Mr Hanrahan was sober that
afternoon and remained downstairs in the front
room, although Mary and Meggie longed for him to
go out so that they could talk openly. Eventually
they retreated to the relative safety of Mary's bedroom, where they conferred in whispers.

'It's a bit scarey,' admitted Mary, who was at last
beginning to come down to earth and wonder how
she was actually going to *face* her mother when the
time came.

'Yeah,' agreed Meggie, 'but it's *good*. This is what
we want. This is the only way we can get away from
Dad. We can tell Mum how awful he's been and
she'll rescue us.'

'Or maybe,' added Mary, 'maybe Mum will realise
what a mess we're all in and she'll come back and
Dad and she will make it up and Dad'll stop drinking.'

'Maybe.'

There was a knock at the front door and the girls
heard Mr Hanrahan go to answer it.

'Uh. Susan,' he said as he opened the door and
Mary sprang to her feet.

'We're up here!' she called down the stairs as she
opened her own door.

'Oh, Hi! Can I come in?'

The question was to Mr Hanrahan, who did not
reply, but let her in grudgingly, slamming the door
behind her.

Quickly, Susan ran up the stairs and joined Mary

and Meggie in the older girl's bedroom.

'Shut the door!' hissed Mary. Susan shut it, then sat down with the other girls on the bed.

'Guess what!' whispered Meggie. 'We've found out where Mum's living!'

'*Have* you?'

'Yes,' continued Mary. 'She's living at 12a Lansdowne Terrace, under an assumed name and Brian's with her and —'

All of a sudden, the door swung open with a crash. Mr Hanrahan was there, towering with fury, his face red, his lips tight, his blue eyes glittering with rage.

'Get out,' he ordered Susan between clenched teeth. 'Get out and never darken my doorstep again.'

Susan trembled and flushed with embarrassment and fear. She dashed from the room and was heard to race down the stairs and out of the house. When the front door closed after her, Mr Hanrahan spoke to his daughters.

'I *knew* you were up to something,' he began, his voice rising to a shout. 'I thought there was something going on behind my back this afternoon and I was right! How dare you! How dare you go against my expressed wishes! You had no business sneaking to your mother behind my back. How *could* you disobey me like that!'

'But she's our mother,' protested Mary lamely. 'Haven't *we* got rights too?'

'You have not!' was the retort. 'You have no rights in this matter whatsoever! This affair is between your mother and me!'

Meggie interrupted. 'But *why* can't we see her?'

'You can't because I say you can't and you need *no other reason*. I daresay *you* are at the back of all this, as usual,' he grunted, glaring at Mary.

'It was both of us!' cried Meggie.

'Bah! Don't bother sticking up for *her*! It's obvious to me she's led you astray. And what was that girl Susan's part in all this, eh?'

'She had no part,' said Mary, frightened. 'I forced her not to tell.'

'Ha! I'm sure she was a willing accomplice.'

'No! She wasn't!'

'I shall have words with her mother about this!'

'Oh no! Please don't!' begged Mary in alarm.

'You'll see the consequences of your bad behaviour!' snapped Mr Hanrahan scornfully. 'You are not to go to that address again, do you hear? Eh?'

The girls hung their heads.

'No, Dad,' was their humbled response.

'If I ever find out that you *have*,' he continued, 'you'll be thrown out of this house, and you can fend for yourselves! Now, we're going next door!'

'Oh no!' pleaded the girls together. 'Please don't! It wasn't Susan's fault!' they implored in vain.

Chapter 27

Consequences

The scene that followed, in the Fellowes' neat, modest front room, was like something out of a TV soap opera. Mrs Fellowes was sitting on their settee, her arm around the shoulders of a sobbing Susan, with Jenny kneeling worriedly on the thin carpet beside them. Mr Hanrahan stood by the one armchair, his arms resolutely folded, his expression fierce. Meggie and Mary were standing behind him, both crying.

'Please sit down, Mr Hanrahan,' urged Jean, still trying to recover from the shock of this sudden drama.

'I shall remain standing,' declared Mr Hanrahan firmly.

'Then I shall stand too,' rejoined Jean who rose to her feet, smoothing her skirt and lifting her chin boldly.

'I want to know,' demanded Mr Hanrahan, 'if you are a party to this scheme to undermine my authority over my own children.'

'I can assure you, this is the first I have ever heard of it,' Jean replied mildly.

'I call it a disgrace!' he burst out. 'I forbid your children ever to enter my house again, or even to *speak* to any of my girls!'

144

'Why?' asked Jean, softly.

Mr Hanrahan was flabbergasted.

'Why?' he repeated. 'Because I say so, that's why! Susan is a deceiver and a liar!'

'Not as a general rule, but she *did* do wrong on this occasion,' admitted Jean. 'I'm very sorry that she had anything to do with this conspiracy. Very sorry. Susan, will you apologise to Mr Hanrahan?'

Susan looked up, her face wet with tears.

'I'm really sorry, Mr Hanrahan,' she sniffed.

This pitiful admission did much to subdue Mary's father and he gave Susan a brief nod of acknowledgment.

'I still forbid you to associate with my daughter,' he insisted nevertheless.

'That's your privilege,' said Jean, 'but I think it would be more adult to simply forget the incident.'

'*I* shan't forget it in a hurry, I can assure you.'

Jean took a deep breath and appeared to be fighting to control her annoyance. 'Listen, Mr Hanrahan,' she began slowly. 'Look at the whole matter from Susan's point of view and from that of your own children. Your girls have been denied access to their own mother for no apparent reason and with no satisfactory explanations given.'

'I have my reasons!' interrupted her opponent.

'Yes, yes, I'm sure you have, but please allow me to continue.'

He tutted impatiently, but continue she did.

'Listen, is it any wonder your girls want to find their mother? You obviously don't want to help them, for your own reasons and if *you* don't want to help them, they're bound to try it themselves if they've got half an ounce of backbone about them, which they evidently have. You ought to be proud of their courage and determination, not to mention their initiative.'

'Rubbish! They disobeyed me and that's all there is to say on the matter.'

'I disagree with you,' countered Jean. 'As far as your children are concerned, there is a great deal on the matter yet to be said.'

'It's no business of yours.'

'It is when my daughter is involved. She is Mary's friend and Mary is short of friends and people she can trust. Mary took Susan into her confidence and Susan did not betray that confidence. Look, I'm not condoning her behaviour by any means and I wish Susan had informed me of what was going on. But I'm sure that now the whole thing is out in the open, Mary and Meggie will not disobey you again and Susan will have no further secrets to keep. So can't we just forget it? Please, Mr Hanrahan.'

'Not on your *life*, my dear woman,' he snorted and, turning on his heel, he left the house, his daughters trailing pathetically behind him. When they had gone, Jean sat down on the settee beside Susan.

'I had to keep the secret,' snivelled the girl as Jean put her arm around her again. 'I had no choice.'

'There, there,' soothed her mother, 'I appreciate how hard it must have been for you, however, we *always* have a choice whether to do right or wrong and I'm afraid you made the wrong choice this time.

Look, if someone tells you to keep a secret that involves them doing something wrong, like, in Mary's case, deceiving her father, you are not *obliged* to agree to keep that secret. Not only are you helping *her* to do wrong, but you're doing wrong yourself. Doing the correct thing is more important than keeping secrets. Do you see?'

Susan sighed and nodded.

'Yes,' she answered. 'I didn't know what to do, though.'

'I know, I know. It's easy to be wise after the event. You live and learn. You know *now* that it was wrong to keep the secret, because you can see the consequences. It's caused bad feeling between our two families and it's made it difficult for you to continue your friendship with Mary.'

'I know,' sniffed Susan. 'Mum, did Mr Hanrahan really mean it when he said I couldn't have anything more to do with her?'

Jean sighed.

'Well ... it sounds as if he did.'

'But that means she can't come to church or Friday Club again.'

'So it seems.'

So it was.

That Sunday morning, Mary was not permitted to go to Gladstone Street and she did not want to go to St Patrick's. She went instead to a small garden centre down the road that was always open on Sundays. Here she wandered aimlessly in the vast greenhouse, among the rows of pot plants and bird tables. The garden centre was busy with other

non-churchgoers choosing seeds, garden ornaments, and bags of peat and fertilizer.

Mary stopped beside a huge display of silk flowers in vases. They made a lovely splash of colour
amongst all the greenery and were all shades
imaginable of pink, red, yellow and blue, and — she
wanted one.

She had no money but, all of a sudden, she was
seized with an irresistible and reckless desire to
steal.

There was no-one watching. She drew closer to
the display, fingering the artificial blooms as if she
were choosing one to buy, looking around her all
the while to check she was not being observed.
Then her hand reached out, grabbed a red carnation, whipped it out of the vase and stuffed it
hurriedly under her jacket. She glanced to either
side of her. No-one had seen. Swiftly, she left the
garden centre and walked home, feeling fearful,
wicked, guilty and triumphant, all at the same time.

Chapter 28

Guilt and Deceit

Mary felt thoroughly bad about herself after that. What was she turning into? What would be the next stage of her gradual worsening as a person?

Only six months ago she had been a well-mannered, well-behaved, clean and pleasant convent schoolgirl. Now, she was surly, disobedient and dishonest. She was a thief, a liar, had been attracted to the 'low life' and was now even a lapsed Catholic. She dressed badly and did not even wash as often as she should, having no mother to supervise her appearance. Added to all that, she was well aware of how awkward and miserable she must appear to others. She felt that the gulf between Mary and normality was widening daily.

Then there were her relationships — how she hated her father and his spoiled, adored Jo! She had little in common, now, with her schoolfriends, who considered her involvement with Gladstone Street to indicate some form of simple-mindedness. She had even lost Susan and her other new friends, now that she was forbidden to associate with them.

There was also the latest cause for grief — the shoplifting incident. She would never have believed herself capable of committing such a crime. Supposing she had been caught? She would have been arrested!

She kept the red, silk carnation in her bedroom, hidden under her bed and, every night, when she was alone in her room, she would bring it out and sit, holding it.

She held the carnation in her hands, with awe and dread. It was like a symbol of herself; cheap, nasty, guilt-ridden, unwanted, even. She had no use for the object and yet she was fascinated by it, because it was something she had stolen. Since she had stolen it, she could not simply throw it away. She knew she would keep it forever, like a memory.

She wanted to make amends for stealing the carnation, so that she could feel completely clean again, but she did not know how to go about it. She was afraid to go to confession. It was so long since she had been to Mass and one of the priests would surely recognise her voice behind the curtain and grille of the confessional box.

She felt that she ought to go back to the garden centre and tell them what she had done, but she feared they might be hard with her and call the police.

She toyed with the idea of trying to return the carnation to the vase, unseen, but thought that if she was seen doing this, they might think she was stealing it instead of putting it back.

She prayed about the matter — directly to God, according to the practice of Gladstone Street. She asked him to forgive her, but had no way of knowing that she was, in fact, forgiven.

She prayed to Our Lady, too, but still felt no better. She felt that the guilt and stain of sin was still upon her.

She decided that she ought to try and be very, very good for the rest of her life, in the hope that God would just forget about the carnation. Even this plan, though, had obvious flaws.

In the first place, she doubted whether she really could be very, very good for the rest of her life and in the second place, how could she know if God really *had* forgotten about it, even after all her efforts?

She resigned herself, in the end, to the knowledge that she was now a second-class person, a sub-human, cursed and tainted. She was scarred for eternity.

In spite of these sentiments, however, Mary still refused to give in to her father's demands regarding her mother. Having obtained the phone number for 12a Lansdowne Terrace, she went several times to a vandal-free call box and each time managed to get through to the house, but with the same unsatisfactory result. Her conversations with the speaker at the other end would proceed thus:

Mary: Hello:
Voice: Yes?
Mary: Is Mrs Powell there please?
Voice: Er ... I'll just go and see.

There would follow a sound of footsteps retreating, a silence and then a sound of advancing feet.

Voice: Er ... I'm afraid she's not in.
Mary: Oh. Do you know when she'll be in?

Voice: Er ... no. Sorry.
Mary: Oh.
Voice: Do you want to leave a message?
Mary: No.

Mary never left a message, because something made her suspect, now, that her mother really was trying to hide from her. She was unavailable too many times for each occasion to be a mere coincidence. The other residents of 12a must have informed her mother, by now, that two children were seeking her. She would realise who those two children were and yet she seemed to show no interest in them. But, Mary reasoned to herself, her mother would not hide from her unless she felt she had to. Perhaps she was afraid that if she contacted her children, that she would get them all into hot water with their father, or perhaps Brian was hiding *her*.

Mary did not tell Meggie that she was still pursuing the search, because she did not want to make trouble for her sister and, of course, she could not continue to take Susan into her confidence. From now on, she was on her own. She knew she would have to revisit the house where her mother lived, because only by turning up there in person could she hope to catch her and she planned to do this as soon as she could. In the meantime, however, she had another task.

Some weeks had elapsed since the inter-family bust-up and the dust had settled. Tempers had cooled. She had been, through fear, very well-behaved at home, always agreeing with her father and doing what she was told as soon as she was told to do it. In short, she had been a model daughter. This altered behaviour evidently pleased her father and their relationship was far less fraught as a result. A lot of the tension was dispelled. They actually had *conversations* these days, about everyday things, without getting into arguments. The ground was well-prepared. So, one evening, as they were watching TV in the front room, Mary was able to ask:

'Dad?'

'Mmm?' he responded, without taking his eyes off the screen.

'Dad, can I go to Gladstone Street again?'

Mary held her breath, as her father looked at her in disbelief.

'You don't still want to go to *that* place, do you?'

'Well, yes,' she admitted. 'I sort of miss it.'

He snorted derisively. 'I forbad you to go there again.'

'Yes — I know that — but —.'

'And I don't like the idea of you being involved with fringe religion. Meggie and Jo have had the good sense not to want to go again.'

Mary sighed, resigning herself to the fact that her cause was lost.

'I just miss it, that's all,' she told him lifelessly.

Her father snorted again and appeared, unusually, uncertain as to what to say next. He fidgeted in his chair, tapping his fingers erratically. Then, to Mary's surprise, he muttered,

'Well, go again if you must. On your own head be

it. I wash my hands off you. I can't say I approve.'

Mary's eyes widened in delight.

'Really!' she exclaimed.

'If you must, but not with my blessing.'

'Oh — great! I mean — thanks, Dad!'

Later that evening, it was his turn to make a request of *her*.

'Mary?' he began, sounding unconvincingly casual.

'Yes, Dad?'

'I hope you don't intend trying to see your mother again.'

'No,' she lied. 'Of course not. Why do you ask?'

'Because I don't want you to do it.'

'Well, I won't.'

'It's for your own benefit, you see,' he continued. 'It's for your own good. I just want to protect you from getting upset, that's all.'

Mary raised an eyebrow, curiously.

'Why should I get upset?' she queried.

'Never you mind,' her father said, 'just do as you're told.'

'Of course,' said Mary.

Chapter 29

Mary Declares Her Intentions

Mary was amazed at her father allowing her to go to Gladstone Street again. It was nothing short of a miracle. She had been expecting an immediate refusal from him and had been so certain of getting it that she had almost not bothered to ask. She was glad, now, that she had.

It was wonderful to be back in the bright, friendly church room with her friends. It felt great to be able to talk freely with Susan again and to meet Dave, Alison and Andy.

'I couldn't believe it when he said yes!' she told them happily as they sat together on the table after Friday Club.

'I'd prayed about it lots,' confessed Susan, with a grin. 'We all prayed you'd be able to come back again.'

'Did you?'

'Yeah,' said Alison. 'We knew your Dad might not let you. That's why we prayed.'

'Well, it worked,' laughed Mary. 'It just *wasn't* what I expected from him! Thanks!'

They continued to chat on about TV programmes and pop groups until Mary saw Pete pass by the open door of the room.

'Oh!' she said, slipping off the table. 'I want to see Pete.'

'What about?' asked Andy.

'I want to get baptised and become a member.'

This unexpected declaration took Mary's friends completely by surprise.

'You *do*?' asked Susan.

'Yes,' smiled Mary.

'Oh.'

Mary's friends, instead of looking pleased, looked bewildered, which puzzled Mary.

'Are you sure?' queried Dave. 'Are you sure you're ready for all that?'

'Of course!' replied Mary confidently. 'I thought about it a lot when I couldn't come to church. Now I'm here again, I want to really join in and be a member. I'll see you later. I want to catch Pete before he goes. Bye!'

With that she left the room, disappointed by her friends' obvious lack of enthusiasm. What was the matter with them? Didn't they *want* her to do the right thing?

She caught up with Pete in the foyer of the church and he greeted her cheerfully.

'Oh, hello Mary,' he said. 'Nice to see you again.'

'It's nice to be back. Can I have a word with you?'

'Yes, sure,' he agreed readily, 'come with me.'

He led her into a small room, furnished with a table and two chairs. It had one, tiny, high window which looked onto the car park.

'Sit down,' he invited, and pulled a chair round for her.

They sat together, on the same side of the table.

'Now, what can I do for you?' he enquired.

'I want to be baptised as a believer and I want to become a member.'

Pete raised both his brows and gave a nervous smile.

'Really,' he said, then appeared to collect his thoughts. 'I see. Right. Well now. Um ... Well, let's start at the beginning. You realise that if you took this step, it'd be a complete break with Catholicism?'

Mary shrugged dismissively.

'I can't be bothered thinking about those things anymore,' she told him. 'All that theology stuff is too complicated. I don't know which denomination is right. All I know is what I want to do.'

'I see. Okay. Why have you asked for believers' baptism, then?'

''Cos I'm a believer, and I want to get baptised,' replied Mary simply.

'Yes. I see,' Pete hesitated. 'Can I ask what it is exactly you believe?'

Mary thought for a moment.

'I believe in God,' she answered at last, 'and in Jesus and all that. I believe it's right to follow Jesus, and to try and be like him — be good, I mean.'

'I see,' said Pete. 'So — how shall I put it — what does Jesus Christ mean to you?'

'He — He's God's Son and He came down to earth to show us the way back to God.'

'How do we get back to God?'

'By obeying the Bible and trying to please Him.'

'I see ... so what does the crucifixion mean to you?'

'Christ died on the cross for us,' answered Mary. 'He died to take away our sins.'

'Fine,' Pete said thoughtfully. 'And has Christ taken away *your* sins, Mary?'

'Yes,' she answered, unable to see the point of the question.

'When did you come to the realisation that Christ died for you, personally?'

This query was also meaningless to Mary.

'I've always known it,' she replied.

'I see ... Let me put it another way. When did you reach a point of repentance — a turning away from living for yourself and deciding to live for Christ?'

Again, Mary did not really understand what he was asking.

'I've always been religious,' she stated. 'Even when I went to the Catholic church, I believed in Christ. Now I want to carry on with my spiritual life — only at Gladstone Street, because I like it better here.'

'Do you?' smiled Pete.

'Yes. It's more friendly. I prefer coming here. I've got friends here now and everyone's really nice. That's why I want to become a member.'

Pete nodded his head, slowly.

'I get the picture,' he said, and rose to his feet.

Mary also rose and he led her to the door.

'Well, you leave it with me,' he concluded, as they left the room and re-entered the foyer. 'I'll speak to the church elders about it and I'll let you know what they say. They'll want to talk to you themselves about it, of course.'

'That's all right,' agreed Mary.

'Good. I really wish I could talk to you a bit more about it myself, now, but I haven't time. I've got to give some of the kids lifts home and if I'm late their parents will wonder where we've got to. But anyway, we'll have another word about it very soon. Okay?'

Mary nodded.

'Yeah, that's fine.'

She went on her way feeling blissfully content, knowing that everything was going to go really well for her from then on. She would become a member of Gladstone Street. God would surely be so pleased with her for having done so that He would forget about the carnation and her other sins. With the support of the other members, her friends, firmly around her, she would be able to fight Dad better and she would have, through Gladstone Street, the love she lacked within her own family.

All these were very comforting ideas, but if Mary thought all her problems were now solved, she was wrong.

Chapter 30

Leave or Stay?

That Sunday, the elders of Gladstone Street had to deal Mary something of a blow. She was still recovering from it, in fact, when she arrived home at Backmount Road with the Fellowes, after church; Neil having driven them home in his car.

'Look, Mary,' said Jean as they stood at their gates, a stiff wind blowing drizzle into their faces. 'Do you need to go indoors right now?'

'No,' answered Mary glumly.

'Then come in for a chat,' Susan's mother urged. 'We can talk about what the elders said.'

'Okay,' agreed Mary, without enthusiasm, as she went into the Fellowes' house with Jean, Jenny and Susan.

Jean went straight through to the kitchen, to put the kettle on. Susan and Mary followed her, while Jenny went upstairs to the bathroom.

'I'm always *desperate* for coffee after church,' Jean told them as she took the jar from the cupboard. 'Aren't you?'

She turned round to look at Mary, but the girl's thoughts were far away. Jean sighed.

'Listen, I know you're upset,' she said consolingly. 'It must seem awfully unreasonable of them.'

'It does!' agreed Mary. 'I thought there would be no problem!'

'Well . . .,' Jean said as she spooned coffee into the mugs. 'It isn't really just a *formality* getting baptised. It isn't just something you do because you want to do it. There's a bit more to it than that, as the elders no doubt explained.'

Mary nodded solemnly.

'They said it was a big step,' she said, 'getting baptised and they said I had to really think about why I was doing it.'

'That's right. It *is* a big step. But you musn't think that they don't *want* you to get baptised. They *do*.'

'Do they?' asked Mary hopefully.

'Of course they do,' put in Susan. 'But they want it to be for the right reasons.'

'I know. I mean, I know what they told me, but I don't really — get it. I feel embarrassed by the whole thing, now. I wish I'd never asked them.'

'Oh no, don't be embarrassed,' Jean said reassuringly. 'They don't mind you *asking*. They're glad you want to join our church, but, as I said before, your motives have to be right.'

Mary shrugged, still feeling foolish, in spite of what Jean had said. In addition, she was rather peeved and offended at the elders' refusal of her application.

'I thought my motives were *fine*,' she insisted. 'I didn't think they'd go on and on about repentance and things. I don't see why I shouldn't be good enough for them as I am.'

'It's not a case of that,' Susan said, keen to make

Mary feel better about the situation. 'It's not a case of you not being good enough.'

Jean handed the girls steaming mugs of hot coffee and they stood to drink it.

'You see,' she explained, 'it's quite reasonable, in one way, to want to get baptised so that you can become a member of Gladstone Street and really feel a part of the church family. I can understand that. The church *is* a family. It's there to support people and it's good that you feel we are your friends. We *are*. Naturally you're going to want to be an official part of it, 'cos you're not the "all take and no give" type. You want to be part of the life of the church, don't you?'

'Yes,' nodded Mary. 'I do.'

'*But*,' continued Jean, 'the thing is that friendship and support are not entirely what the church is for. The church is a fellowship of believers. Do you know what that means?'

Mary was not sure.

'Does it mean,' she suggested, 'people believing the same things — having the same faith?'

'Yes,' agreed Jean, 'and that's the snag, as far as really "joining in" is concerned. You have to be born again — that's what Jesus ordained. You have to have undergone a *change* — deep down in your soul. You need to have realised how you stand before God — as a sinner, needing to be saved. You need to realise that you're very far away from God and that you can only get near to Him by accepting Christ as your Saviour. If Christ is not your Saviour, you have no hope of heaven.'

Mary felt a twinge of annoyance. She didn't like it when Jean, or anyone else, went on about being saved like this. They were trying to suggest that if she didn't go all 'Jesus-freakish' like they were, then she wasn't really a Christian. She knew this was nonsense. She wasn't really a sinner. Of course, she did feel guilty about the shoplifting, and about hating her father and Jo, but — well, if Dad and Jo weren't so awful then she wouldn't hate them, and if Dad didn't make her so unhappy then she wouldn't have to steal from shops. If he was decent to her then she wouldn't be forced to lie to him. If he gave her money then she wouldn't need to steal from him, and if she had a mother then she'd be a nicer person altogether.

If anyone was going to be Mary's 'saviour' it was her mother. Once Mum came home to sort everything out, then Mary would go back to being the person she had used to be. Once Mum came home, Mary wouldn't need Gladstone Street anymore.

'It would be a good idea,' Jean continued, interrupting Mary's train of thought, 'if you read through that booklet Pete gave you. It explains things quite well, better than I can.'

Mary fished out the booklet from her pocket. It was entitled 'God's Gift' and had a photograph of a cross, in silhouette, on the front cover. She flicked through it. It was full of Bible verses.

'Yeah, I suppose I'll read it sometime,' she told Jean, knowing all the while that she probably would not.

'Good,' smiled Susan's mother. 'Maybe, after

you've thought about it, you'll understand what we mean when we say that the most important thing in your life is how you stand before God.'

There was a pause, while each of the three drank their coffee and pondered their separate thoughts: Jean and Susan, both concerned, that they should be understood, without putting Mary off, and Mary, beginning to plan the rest of her afternoon.

'I must go now,' she said, quickly downing what remained of her coffee and placing the empty mug on the table. 'Things to do. See you.'

Jean and Susan both looked slightly dismayed at Mary's haste to depart.

'Do you feel all right about things, now?' queried Susan, sounding worried.

'Yeah. Fine,' answered Mary, distantly, as the two girls went through to the front door.

'Are you coming to church this evening?' pursued her friend.

'Might do,' replied Mary. 'Bye.'

With this she left.

When she had gone, Susan returned to her mother in the kitchen. Jean appeared pensive.

'Mum,' began Susan, 'I think we upset Mary.'

Jean did not answer, but gave an unhappy sigh as she busied herself preparing their dinner.

'Do you think she's gone off us?' continued the girl, twiddling nervously with a lock of her mousey hair.

'I don't know,' answered Jean, with concern. 'The elders were right, though, to make her stop and think before getting baptised. It's obvious that Mary needs to approach the matter carefully and sort out her beliefs first.'

'But perhaps we should just baptise people without asking questions. Then people wouldn't get offended.'

'No,' said Jean, with a decisive shake of the head. 'We'd be doing them no favours if we did that. Jesus never lulled folk into a false sense of security and neither should we. He said He had come not to bring peace, but a sword. Some things are hard to say, but they have to be said. Sometimes it's as hard for us to say them as it is for others to hear.'

'That's true all right,' assented Susan. 'The last thing I want to do is put Mary off coming to Gladstone Street, just when she's started coming back.'

'I know, but maybe this is all part of God's plan for Mary. Maybe this is God's way of making her *listen* to what He has to say.'

Susan looked bewildered.

'What I mean,' explained Jean, 'is that Mary can't just carry on now at Gladstone Street as she has been doing. This morning has made her stop and think about our church in a way she didn't before. She's had to stop thinking about it as a group of friends and start thinking about it in spiritual terms. She isn't stupid. She just won't forget what was said to her — the personal challenge. She'll make a decision about it. She'll either accept or reject the gospel.'

'And then what?' asked Susan. 'What if she rejects it?'

Jean considered her reply.

'If she rejects the gospel,' she said at last, 'she'll do one of two things. She'll either carry on coming to Gladstone Street and put the spiritual side of it out of her mind, or she'll decide not to come anymore.'

'Oh,' said Susan, dismayed. 'What do *you* think she'll do if she rejects it?'

Jean grimaced.

'We can only pray about it,' she said.

Chapter 31

The Encounter

Mary's mind was not on Gladstone Street, or the Fellowes, as she made the now-familiar bus journey to Bromley after lunch. It was a grey, cold day and a fine rain had been falling since noon. The top deck of the bus smelled of stale cigarette smoke and damp raincoats, and Mary was chilled in her wet anorak.

She was not in the mood for adventure. The first two trips, with Meggie, to Bromley had been exciting and the girls had been full of expectation as they travelled, but, this time, Mary felt, instead, a taste of the 'dread-full-ness' she had experienced when she had first learned of her parents' break-up. It was because the novelty of the quest had worn off and because she was afraid of meeting her mother again after such a long interval. She was afraid, too, of not being welcomed by her mother, for whatever reason.

She had so much to tell her; so many questions to ask and she was as reluctant to hear the answers, as she had been when she asked Danielle about her mother all those months ago. She did not want to hear all the sordid details of her parents' marriage, but she had to find them out nevertheless.

167

She tried to imagine what the conversation with her mother would be like.

She would ring the appropriate doorbell of 12a Lansdowne Terrace and, after a few moments, her mother's shape would become visible behind the glass of the front door.

Her mother would open the door and Mary would say: 'Hello, Mum.'

Her mother would look shocked at first, then pleased. She would say: 'Mary! You've found me! How did you know where to find me!'

'I found the address in your diary.'

'Oh Mary,' Mum would say. 'I've missed you so much.'

Then they would embrace and Mary would smell the well-remembered, warm, perfumed fragrance of her mother's skin. They would be re-united; able to love each other again and all would be well.

Her mother would take Mary upstairs to — Mary had to invent a description of the flat — to a small, clean, comfortable, little apartment. Brian would be, conveniently, absent. Mary and her mother would sit on Mum's single bed, their arms around each other and they would talk. Mary would tell her mother how awful things were with Dad, how unhappy they all were, and Mum would say, horrified:

'Mary! I had no idea! What happened to all the money I sent your father?'

'What money?' Mary would ask.

'The money I gave him each week to help look after you.'

'I don't know anything about it.'

'Oh no! He must have spent it all on himself! To think he actually let you go hungry!'

'We do go hungry, Mum.'

'And he's drunk? Every night?'

'Yes, Mum.'

They would cuddle closer together and Mum would smooth Mary's hair, as she rested her head on the familiar, soft shoulder.

'Oh, if only I'd known,' Mum would say regretfully. 'If only I'd known how bad things were, nothing would have stopped me from finding you. My poor darling. I'm so sorry. So very sorry.'

Mary would begin to weep tears of joy and sadness.

'Why didn't you take us with you, Mum?' she would ask. 'Why didn't you take us with you when you left?'

'He wouldn't let me,' she would explain. 'He said I wasn't fit to care for you, because of my involvement with Brian.'

'But why are you involved with Brian, Mum?' Mary would ask.

Mum would sigh deeply.

'Brian loves me,' she would say sorrowfully. 'Your father loves the bottle more than he ever loved me. He was cruel, so cruel. I could stand it no longer. I had to leave. Brian offered me a way out, so I took it. But I've not been happy. I've missed you, Meggie and Jo so much.'

'Then why didn't you try to find us?'

'I was afraid of your father; afraid of what he

might do to me if I came near you. I was so sure that you would be all right as I thought he was capable of caring for you, with Danielle's help. I had no idea he would let himself go like that!'

'So will you help us now?' Mary would plead.

'Of course, of course,' her mother would reply. 'What do you think would be the best thing to do? Shall I take you away from him? We could make a new family with Brian.'

Mary would shake her head quickly.

'No!' she would protest. 'I love Dad, don't you?'

Mary was unsure as to how her mother would answer this question. Perhaps she might say:

'Yes, of course I love him.'

This was the best answer.

Then Mum might say:

'I'll come back home with you. Brian will understand. We'll try again, your father and me.'

'Yes!' Mary would agree, eagerly. 'He'll stop drinking then, won't he?'

'Yes. He will. Then we will be happy. He won't be cruel to me again, because he'll have learnt his lesson. There now, how does that sound?'

Mary would glow with pleasure. It sounded just perfect.

Suddenly, she woke up from her daydream. The bus had halted at her stop and she had to get off quickly.

She hurried down the steps of the double-decker and jumped off. Turning up the collar of her damp anorak against the rain, she walked rapidly along the shiny pavement, under the dripping trees, until she arrived at the iron gate of 12a.

It creaked open at her touch. She crunched up the gravel of the drive, past the red Mini, to the front door, with its three bells.

She rang the top one and heard it buzz somewhere towards the roof of the house. There was no sound of footsteps to signal that anyone had heard. She rang the next bell down. Again, there was no reply. Then she rang the final bell and heard a door opening. A shape appeared behind the glass. A black-haired young man in a leather jacket opened the front door.

'Yeah?' he said, absently.

'Is Mrs Powell at home?'

'Mrs Powell? From the top flat?'

'Yes.'

'Did you ring her bell?'

'Yes.'

'Then she's not here, if she didn't answer it.'

'Oh. No.'

'She's behind you.'

'What?'

Mary wheeled round and looked back down the drive.

'That's her, at the gate,' said the young man.

It was.

Mary's mother was standing at the iron gate, about to push it open. She noticed Mary and froze, like a hunted animal. Her brown eyes stared at her daughter momentarily, then narrowed as Mary ran towards her. She remained on the pavement side of the gate, her dark hair glistening with rain-drops, her skin tanned, her lips red. She was wearing a new skirt-suit, chocolate-coloured.

'Mum!' cried Mary, the tears starting to her eyes. 'Mum!'

Her mother looked anxious.

'Hello Mary,' she said, politely.

'*Mum!*'

There was an explosive silence. All of a sudden, Mary's rehearsed questions had deserted her.

'How are you, Mary?' asked her mother, with the same air of coolness.

'I'm fine!' exclaimed Mary, her emotions wild with the thrill of the longed-for encounter.

'Oh Mum! I'm so pleased to see you!'

Mary's mother did not smile in response. She said, 'I'm surprised you managed to find me.'

'It took ages! Oh, Mum!'

Mary held out her arms to her mother and her mother received the hug, returning it briefly, as if she were a distant relation.

'Mum, you must come home!' said Mary.

Her mother shook her head.

'I can't,' she said.

Mary was stunned.

'Why?' she asked, breathlessly.

'I can't, that's all,' replied her mother. 'I've started a new life now, with Brian.'

'A new life?' repeated Mary with disbelief.

'Yes. Now, I really must get on.'

Mary's mother pushed open the gate, forcing her

daughter to take a step back. She stepped onto the drive in her high heels and started to walk, briskly, to the front door, as if she expected Mary to leave.

'MUM!'

Mary went after her and came alongside her mother, but her mother still did not look at her.

'Mum! Wait!' she called, panicking. 'There are things I want to ask you! There are things I want to know!'

Mary's mother ignored the request and entered the house through the still-open front door. She turned around to close it, saying, 'please don't bother me again. What happened between your father and I is none of your business. I've started a new life. I'm not prepared to talk about my reasons for doing so. Please go now.'

She closed the door, firmly.

Mary was left on the doorstep, dripping wet.

There were no answers, no explanations.

She had no rights.

She had nothing.

Chapter 32

Trust

Mary stood on the doorstep for a long time, not knowing what to do. She rang her mother's doorbell, but her mother did not answer it. In the end, Mary realised that there was no point in staying. It was obvious that her mother really did not want to see her daughter again.

She went back down the drive and out of the gate, closing it behind her. Then she took a last look at the house, and at the blank windows of the top flat, before walking away. She would never return. She would never pester her mother again.

In the pouring rain, Mary walked away from Bromley, feeling cold, with her hair dripping and her clothes soaked. She walked back to the seedy suburb where she lived and to the dirty, mean streets that her mother would never know. She trudged up the littered hill to her home in Backmount Road and entered the disorderly, filthy house.

She was here for keeps, now. Mum was not going to rescue her daughters and take them away to a better existence in a prettier part of town. They would not enjoy security again, or plenty. Mary and her sisters were stuck with poverty, drunkenness, squalor and hatred, until they grew up and could leave.

She went straight to her room and stayed there, going over and over again in her mind what had occurred at Lansdowne Terrace. She could not believe it had happened. She could not believe it had been so final and so brutal.

The lady called Mrs Powell had been her mother. She had borne her, had nursed her, had watched her grow up, learn to walk and talk, and start school, and now — it was as if her mother had forgotten every one of all those years. It was as if she had forgotten every kiss, every tear, every small event that forms fond recollection. None of it mattered to Mrs Powell. Mrs Powell was starting a new life and the past was left with those who wished to remember it.

Mary did not tell Meggie what had happened. She saw no reason why Meggie should be hurt.

For days, she kept herself to herself, and hardly spoke. It was the school holidays, so she did not have to leave the house if she did not want to. And she did not want to.

It was easy to keep the reason for her silence from her sisters and from Dad. Dad was not at home enough to notice it anyway and her sisters assumed that she was merely in a bad mood.

The truth was, the only mood she experienced was one of hopelessness and all her other feelings were numbed. Her grief was beyond tears and her solitude so deep that she did not feel the need for company.

Susan broke into her self-imposed loneliness on the Friday, when she called at the house to see if Mary wanted to go to Friday Club. Meggie answered the door.

'Oh, she's in her room,' she replied to Susan's question. 'She's got the sulks. Go on up if you want.'

'Okay.'

Susan came in and went up the stairs to Mary's bedroom, knocking timidly at the door rather than walking straight in. As far as Susan was concerned, Mary's mood was due to the events of the previous Sunday morning, regarding her friend's request for baptism. She knew nothing of what had happened since.

'Come in,' Mary said reluctantly.

Susan entered the room with caution and sat down on the bed beside her friend.

'A — are you coming to Friday Club?' she queried hopefully.

'No,' said Mary.

'Oh ... Why?'

'I don't want to.'

Susan sighed worriedly.

'Look, if it's about what happened on Sunday —.'

Mary looked sharply at her.

'How do you know?' she asked, not realising what Susan was referring to.

Susan looked puzzled.

'How do I know what?' she questioned innocently.

'How do *you* know what happened?'

'Eh? What do you mean?'

'I haven't told anyone!' Mary said, equally bewildered.

'What about?'

The penny suddenly dropped then with Mary. She turned her eyes away from Susan and said, 'Oh, you think I'm upset about that baptism stuff.'

'Yes. Aren't you?'

'That's the least of my worries.'

'Then what is it?' persisted Susan anxiously. 'Has something else happened?'

Mary hesitated.

'No,' she said.

Susan did not believe her.

'Something has happened, hasn't it?' she asked. 'Come on, tell me, what's wrong?'

'No. I'm tired. Go away.'

Susan looked hurt, and rose.

'I'll go then,' she suggested.

'Yes. Bye.'

So Susan left.

When she had gone, Mary wished she had not asked her to leave. She was suddenly seized with an urge to call her back and tell her everything, but it was too late.

The desire to talk, however, did not leave Mary once it had arrived. She did not go to church on Sunday, but, choosing an hour when she knew the Fellowes would be at home, she left her own house for the first time in a week and went next door.

Jean let her in and led her into the Fellowes' cosy front room, where Susan and Jenny were sitting, reading magazines.

'Do you want a coffee?' enquired Jean gently, as Mary seated herself, rather stiffly, on an armchair.

'No, thank you.'

Jean sat down on the hearthrug and the family all looked at Mary, who stared into her lap.

'Now, how can we help you?' asked Jean.

Mary swallowed, took a deep breath and told them everything that had happened to her in Bromley the previous Sunday.

Only when she came to the bit where her mother closed the door in her face did she start to cry and, as she began to cry, she started to 'let go' for the first time in a week. For the first time in a week, she let her pent-up feelings be known and communicated to the outside world the sorrow and loneliness that had been eating her up inside.

Hot tears flowed down her cheeks and her thin body shook with sobbing.

'She doesn't want us . . .,' she told Susan, Jean and Jenny, who had gathered closely around her. Susan held her hand and Jean had her arms around Mary's trembling shoulders.

'Mum doesn't love us anymore ... She doesn't care what happens to us.'

'Poor Mary . .,'was all Jean and Susan could say, but they meant it and Mary appreciated the fact that they cared, when her own mother did not.

'I don't understand,' went on Mary. 'How could she not love us anymore? How could she just turn her back on us?'

'I don't know,' answered Jean honestly. 'I just don't know.'

'She gave no reasons. She wouldn't tell me anything. I'll never know now. I'll never know the truth. I'll never know *why*.'

'No,' sighed Jean, sympathetically. 'Maybe you never will.'

'I don't know what we've *done*,' cried Mary, sniffing and wiping her nose on her sleeve. 'I don't know what Meggie, Jo and I have done, for her not to love us. And Dad doesn't care. He doesn't love us either. We're just a burden to him. No-one loves us. No-one wants us.'

'That's not true,' Jean stated firmly.

'Yes it is.'

'No. It isn't. There is one who wants to love you.'

'What?'

'Mary, God loves His children.'

'He's got a funny way of showing it,' was her bitter response.

'No, no. Listen. Just listen a minute. Please. Will you?'

Mary looked up at Jean with tear-blurred vision.

'All right,' she said, out of politeness.

Jean held Mary's free hand as she began to talk.

'Mary,' she said, 'can you see what you've been doing? You thought your Mum would be the answer to all your problems, didn't you? You put her on a pedestal. You thought that *she* was what you needed. You depended upon her utterly for help and survival. You relied upon her love. You trusted her to always love and care for you. Didn't you?'

'Of course.'

'You thought that she would always be there for

you and she wasn't.' Jean gave a sad sigh. 'Oh, Mary, love, no one person can be relied upon to be always there, never changing. People are mortal. They can't *always* be trusted and they can't *always* help. You can't depend upon them absolutely to be everything you want them to be. Do you understand?'

'Yes,' answered Mary quietly, 'I've learned that now.'

'But there is one who never changes, who never stops loving and who is always there to help. You know who I mean.'

'You mean God.'

'Yes. I mean God. He will never fail. He will never forsake you and you can be sure of that in a way that you can never be sure of any one human being.'

'But He can't really help me,' objected Mary.

'He *can*,' insisted Jean. 'He can if only you become one of His adopted children. He can if you are one of His family.'

Mary shook her head.

'How can I *know* that,' she said. 'How can I *know* He loves me?'

Chapter 33

Mary Makes a Decision

Jean did not explain right away. She told Mary it would be better to talk about it when she was feeling calmer and could think straight.

Mary went away from the Fellowes that afternoon, feeling comforted, at least, and loved. She was able to carry that feeling with her back home, like a warm cocoon. Jean had counselled her not to tell her family yet about having found her mother and Mary was happy to take that advice. She did not feel up to another verbal battering, caused by a conflict with her father.

The crisis that had just passed proved to be a turning point for Mary. All faith in her mother as protector and friend having been proven ill-founded, she began to search for the love of God in a way she had never done before. Her mother had been Mary's last remaining emotional crutch and now that crutch had been knocked away, there was only one 'parent' left to turn to. So she turned to Him.

Over the next few weeks, Jean and Susan showed her the way.

Mary went to church and Friday Club, and a strange thing began to happen to her. The Bible, which had before been a dry and dull book, suddenly became alive and the words seemed to shine out from the page, with new interest and relevance. Suddenly, she was reading the Bible with as much enthusiasm as if it were a best-selling novel. Every day she read chapters and chapters of it, marvelling at what she learned, especially from the book of Romans. She read 'God's Gift', the booklet that she had been given that fateful Sunday and was startled at what it contained. She re-read it again and again, committing herself to the truth within it over and over.

She knew she must have heard it all before — the gospel, but somehow, it was as if she had never *really* heard it before and was understanding it for the first time. As she took it all in, she grew as excited and thrilled by what she read as if it were the most important and best bit of news she had ever heard.

She learned for the first time that she needed Christ to be her Saviour and that her sins had separated her from her God. She found out that God would not just forget about her sins — He would not just forget about the stolen carnation, or about her hatred for her father and Jo, or about her lies, or about the money she stole. She could never hope to make it up to God by spending hours in prayer, or by trying to be good, or even by being very sorry.

There was only one way she could satisfy God and make sure that she was loved by Him. That was by trusting in Christ and in His shed blood alone, for the complete forgiveness of her sins. There was only one way she could be part of God's family. That was by loving Him and loving Him meant believing what He said in His Word, the Bible, and showing her faith through obedience. She learned that she had to live *for* Christ and *in* Christ and turn her back on her own wants and wishes.

Once all this was revealed to her, everything changed. The load of guilt she had been carrying regarding her thefts, lies and hatreds seemed to slip from her shoulders. She *knew* that God had forgiven her, through Christ. She knew that His forgiveness was complete and that she did not have to add to it in any way by anything she did, other than trusting Him. She could be *sure* that, as far as God was concerned, the sins really were forgotten, for ever. She was born again, a true Christian at last.

The guilt and worry became replaced with joy and gratitude, and love for her Heavenly Father. As God turned from being a distant, remote figure into her personal friend, she began to enjoy a measure of security and comfort, and a sense of never being completely alone.

As her knowledge of God increased and her love for Him grew, she quickly found herself wanting to find ways to please Him and she began to drop old, bad habits. She stopped stealing from her father. This meant that she was no longer in control of her money supply, but, somehow, she always seemed to manage. She received anonymous gifts of cash from the church and, curiously, her father began to be more generous.

She stopped being so cheeky to him, though she

did, occasionally, lapse, and she stopped lying to him. This did not make him cease taking advantage of her, or cease being unpleasant and unreasonable from time to time, but it did change some things. By avoiding arguments and the subsequent regrets, Mary felt happier about herself and this had the effect of making it easier for her to forgive him when he wronged her. She wasn't sure exactly *how* it made forgiveness easier, but it did. Her relationship with him less fraught, she did not feel so agitated about him all the time and began to be able to regard him with a certain detachment. For the first time since their family had broken up, she began to understand what made him so angry, so depressed and so unhappy. In the light of this understanding, her hatred diminished, though it still flared up when she was provoked.

She began to be nicer to Jo. She learned to appreciate her younger sister's difficulties, to be gentle with her and more patient. The relationship improved as a result, which made the atmosphere in the house better and turned Jo and her into friends, where before they had been enemies.

Meggie and Jo both noticed these changes in their sister's behaviour, following her conversion, even though she did not tell them that anything had happened to her until weeks after it had. Although she was filled with the joy and excitement of becoming a Christian, for some reason she was nervous about telling others what had happened to her.

After a while, though, she gained a little confidence and spoke out. Meggie was the first person she shared her faith with: she did not attempt to explain things to Jo, who was still very young.

Mary guessed, rightly, that Meggie would be relatively easy to talk to, as the sisters were close and Meggie could be expected to remain a friend, even if she did not think much of what Mary believed. She still found it difficult, however, to pluck up the courage to talk to her. Mary knew that she ran a risk of driving a wedge, however small, between them.

An opportunity to share her faith came one Sunday, soon after Mary's conversion.

The girls had just shared a lunch of crisps and spam. Jo was sitting on the front room floor, fascinated by a black-and-white film on the TV. Dad was not expected home for another hour at least.

'Meggie,' began Mary tentatively. She was trying to sound casual. 'Do you fancy going to Gladstone Street again? Jenny keeps asking me why you don't go anymore.'

The truth was that Jenny no longer expected to see Meggie at church, as she had not attended for several weeks, but Mary felt she had to justify her question somehow, since it came out of the blue.

Her sister answered, with little interest:

'Nah. I'm not bothered about church now.'

'Why not?' enquired Mary.

'I got bored with it, that's all.'

There was a pause, while Mary wondered how to prolong the conversation.

'I really love it,' she went on at last. 'It's really made me *think*, y'know?'

Mary hoped, by this remark, to prompt Meggie to

say, 'has it?' Or else something equally helpful. If Meggie said, 'has it?' Mary would be able to tell her precisely what it was she found so interesting. Meggie's curiousity, however, was not aroused, so Mary was forced to continue unassisted.

'The things I've learned about *Jesus* are just incredible,' she said. 'Things I never knew before.'

At the mention of the name 'Jesus' Mary observed her sister tense slightly, as if she had just said something offensive. Mary could understand Meggie's reaction. Before her conversion the mention of the name 'Jesus' would have produced exactly the same reaction in herself. Now, of course, the name was wonderful to her, but it was not so with Meggie. The introduction of 'Jesus' into the conversation made dull, old black-and-white films on the TV suddenly interesting and Meggie fixed her eyes on the screen intently.

'It's brilliant what Jesus has done,' continued Mary nevertheless. She tried to cover her nerves by sounding enthusiastic, but she knew she sounded apologetic. 'When I read my Bible —.'

Meggie tutted loudly at the word 'Bible' and gave her sister a withering look.

'I get embarrassed when people go on about God and — *Jesus*, like that,' she informed Mary irritably. 'Jenny used to do it all the time and now *you*'re at it! You're *always* reading your Bible these days.'

Mary was taken aback. She had not expected *quite* such a bad reaction as this.

'But you never used to *mind* when Jenny talked about Jesus.'

Meggie shrugged.

'I do *now*,' she said bluntly. 'I find it really embarrassing *now*.'

'Oh.'

Mary 'chickened out' of her witness at this point. It was obvious that she must have been 'sharing her faith' with Meggie all along, just by having a Bible around and just by being different. Meggie had obviously drawn her own conclusions from these clues, before Mary uttered a word.

It was uncanny, the effect of the name of Jesus. Mary was to find that, in the future, *that name* always produced the same response from her sister. *That name* became a barrier between the two of them. Although, in all other respects, their relationship remained a good one, Mary found that when Meggie was in a bad mood with her, she called her 'Jesus Freak', or 'Born-again', using Christianity as a term of abuse. If their roles had been reversed, Mary knew that she would have done exactly the same thing, but it still hurt and made her feel isolated and sad.

However, there was worse to come. Mary had yet to witness to her father.

Chapter 34

The Challenge

Mary knew that she had to share her faith with her father and she desperately wanted to do so. Her knowledge of God and of His plan of salvation was such a vital and important revelation to her that she longed for her Dad to understand and believe it.

If he became a Christian, it would make such a big difference to him. He would have something to be happy about, like Mary had, and some comfort and reassurance to counter all the disruption and disappointment in his life. Dad, if he came to faith in the Lord, would know that although his wife might not care for him any more, that God *did* and that God loved him even more than his wife had ever done. Dad would also come to the realisation that God could console his grief much better than beer or whisky and, once he realised that, he would be bound to stop drinking, because he would not feel he needed it anymore.

Mary also knew that Dad would have to have saving faith in order to have his sins forgiven. If he did not trust in the blood of Christ, then his sins were still upon him and if his sins were still upon him, then he would go to hell when he died. Mary did not want to think of Dad spending eternity in hell: that would be terrible. She had to help him repair his life and get right with God.

The question was, how? Her attempt to tell Meggie about the gospel had shown her that it was no easy task. When would be the right moment to talk to Dad about it? How would he react? How could she make him understand that 'Christian' was not a title you acquired as a baby?

It was scarey. Although it was something she really wanted to do, she wanted just as much to feel *able* to do it and she wasn't sure she *was* able. She didn't want to lay herself open to yet another blasting from him, not even for the best of reasons. She did not want to expose herself to his ridicule and scorn, and she did not want to provide him with something to taunt her with in the future. And yet, she was forced to accept that he might react that way. It might prove to be the 'kiss of death' to their relationship, which was already frayed at the edges. *Or*, she knew she ought not to be so pessimistic, it might turn them into the best of friends for the rest of their lives. Mary had no way of predicting the outcome.

She prepared for it by spending a long time in prayer up in her room, on the Thursday evening when she decided to speak to him. She had told Alison, Susan, Andy and Dave what she planned to do that night and she took comfort in the knowledge that, at that moment, they were praying for her.

Meggie was upstairs, doing her homework, at the time and Jo was in bed.

It was a dark, rainy October night and Dad was having a rare, sober, evening in front of the TV. Neglecting her French essay, which also had to be fitted in, somehow, Mary went downstairs from her room to join him.

The curtains of the stuffy, front room were drawn crookedly and the gas fire hissed, full on. Her father was watching a chat show.

Mary sat down, carefully, on the settee and pretended to become engrossed in the chat show, in order to appear relaxed. She and Dad commented on the guests and the host, and she succeeded in generating a friendly, easy atmosphere between them. Privately, though, her tension was increasing by the minute and she was sweating in the hot room. She was panicking, too. She didn't know how she was going to broach the subject and yet it really was now or never.

In the end, quite abruptly, she burst out, 'Dad? Dad — I've become a Christian.'

Mr Hanrahan appeared, understandably, uncomprehending and turned to look at her, sharply.

'You've *what*?' he asked, though it was obvious he had heard her quite clearly.

Mary attempted a smile.

'I've become a Christian,' she repeated timorously.

'What do you mean by *that*?' her father demanded, rapidly becoming, to Mary's consternation, as tense as she was herself.

'I mean I've been saved. Christ has died for me and saved me from hell,' Mary explained, knowing that the words would mean nothing at all to her father.

'Saved you from hell?' he repeated derisively. 'What on *earth* are you talking about?'

'I've been born again,' Mary said.

This was going from bad to worse. She had managed to choose precisely the 'wrong' words.

'*Born again?*' repeated her father, scornfully. Then he gave a short laugh. He seemed genuinely amused. '*Born again*? That's what those wretched — what do you call 'em — those American TV evangelists call themselves, isn't it?' He blasphemed incredulously. 'Born again, born again! Whatever next!'

'But Dad, it's got nothing to do with America,' insisted his daughter imploringly. 'It's a word in the Bible —.'

'The *Bible*! Good grief!' He laughed again. 'What are you turning into! The *Bible*! Ha! Is this all from that Susan — what's her name —.' He pretended he could not remember her surname, as a token of his lack of esteem for the girl. ' — This is all from *that* family, isn't it?'

'Yes — I mean — *no!*' floundered Mary. She had forgotten to rely on the help of the Holy Spirit within her to help her through her witness and she had lost her confidence as a result. 'It's not because of *them*. It's to do with *me*. This is *my* faith.'

'*Your* faith! But you're a Catholic!'

'Not any more,' admitted Mary fearfully.

'You mean you're a *Protestant*?' rejoined her father in disbelief.

Mary hesitated to answer.

'Er — yes — but — but that's not really the point — I'm a Christian. That's what I really —.'

'A Protestant,' continued her father, relentlessly pursuing his own train of thought, 'you've turned into a Protestant.' He shook his head in a gesture of resignation and disgust. 'This is a *Catholic* family,' he insisted. 'How dare you dispense with the faith of your fathers and of your ancestors? Why — Catholics have been *martyred* rather than renounce their faith — and yet *you* —.' He blasphemed again.

'But Dad — it's not that I —.'

But her father was not listening. He did not want to listen to her explanations. He was not really interested in his daughter's spiritual status. Denominations were his chief concern and loyalties; politics, even. He lectured her for half an hour on Northern Ireland and the Easter Rising of 1916, and then sent her to bed.

If Mary had helped herself by being better behaved to her father, this help was all but cancelled out by her conversion and witness. He despised her for it. This made Mary feel sad, but he did not succeed in making her feel *bad*. She had been warned that all Christians have to suffer in some way because of their faith, but she knew it was a small price to pay.

It was a small price to pay for everything that she had gained. It was worth it all for the sake of knowing that God was her Protector and Jesus

Christ her Brother. It was worth the hardship to know that her Heavenly Father would always take care of her and always provide for her every need. Such security and peace of mind were worth holding on to. Mary knew that whatever family life threw at her, nothing could take away the joy that now lightened her face and gave her hope for the future, where before there had been only hopelessness.

She relied more and more on Gladstone Street. Now that she was spiritually in tune with them, she was able to reap the benefits of fellowship to the full. Her circle of friends widened and she never lacked the love and support that she needed.

She needed Alison, Susan, Andy and Dave especially now, because Jill and Clare at St Columba's became even more estranged from her when she shared her faith with *them*. Jill and Clare thought she was weird and they told everyone else she was weird, which was really hard to bear. Mary felt very lonely at school, now.

She lived for her weekends, for socialising with her Christian friends and for Sundays with Christian families, who invited her out to lunch. Meggie and Jo envied Mary her Sunday lunches, if nothing else.

The company of other Christians was essential to her. Without it, as at school or home, she would feel sometimes as if she were the only Christian on earth. When she was *with* her Christian friends, she enjoyed a depth of friendship and trust that she had never experienced *anywhere* before, not even within her own family. This special kind of love was something she treasured.

Because she was human, though, she still worried about things.

She wondered how she could continue to cope with the isolation and loneliness of school. She was to attend St Columba's for another four years, after all. Mary knew she was on a sort of spiritual 'high' now, soon after her conversion and that this gave her the energy to cope, but what would she feel like if that energy disappeared and becoming a Christian was no longer a novelty? Would she be able to keep her faith going, when she had so much opposition to contend with?

There were other questions, too. *Mum* had not heard the gospel. Should Mary try and get in touch with her?

Then there were the more long-term questions. She did not know if she would ever escape Backmount Road, or her father. Would she live the rest of her life in squalor and poverty, with the odour of stale beer in her nostrils? She hoped not.

She wondered if she would ever get a boyfriend and marry. Would she find someone who not only liked *her*, but loved God?

If she thought too much about the future, she became anxious. Anyway, it was pointless worrying. Mary continually reminded herself that her future was no longer her concern: it was God's. She had given her future over to Him and she knew that the rest of her life was in His hands. Because God loved her, she could trust Him to make sure she had the strength to handle whatever was to come. Nothing would happen to her that she could not bear.

It seemed to Mary that the rest of her days lay before her like a strange, mist-shrouded landscape. She did not know what to expect ahead of her; whether her future would be dominated by joy or sorrow. In that respect she was like any other girl, but she knew that in one important respect she was not.

The old Mary would have had to journey into the future alone, with no-one to guide her and no promise of help. For the different Mary, however, this was not so.

She would never have to journey alone.

'The pain was searing and intense. She screwed up her eyes and clenched her teeth, she was determined not to scream'.

Helen was only 15 when the soldiers came to the farm and tortured her. But she gave away no secrets. The farmer's hiding-place was safe with her.

This story takes place during a cruel and violent time in Scotland's history — and tells about the faith of a girl and her brother as they stand up against evil people who try to stop them worshipping God.

FOCUS

Helen of the Glen

to Triumph

George F. Maclean

The Young Christian

Matthew Henry

Using Paul's letter to Titus, Matthew Henry here shows us how best to live as a Christian. There is no shortage of books today claiming to tell us how to live a full life but Henry makes it clear that the Christian way is the right way.

He deals with the company we keep, the books we read, and many other practical issues which still face every Christian.

'A life spent in the service of God, and communion with him, is the most comfortable life anyone can live in this world.'

Any reader of *The Young Christian* will see clearly how concerned Henry was that young believers would realise the truth of his words, spoken after a lifetime of service.